FURY'S LADY

STEPHANIE WEBB DILLON

Copyright © 2024 by Stephanie Webb Dillon

All rights reserved.

No part of this publication may be reproduced, distributed, or transmitted in any form or by any means, including photocopying, recording, or other electronic or mechanical methods, without the prior written permission of the publisher, except as permitted by U.S. copyright law. For permission requests, contact [include publisher/author contact info].

The story, all names, characters, and incidents portrayed in this production are fictitious. No identification with actual persons (living or deceased), places, buildings, and products is intended or should be inferred.

Cover model: Alfie Gordillo

Photographer: Reggie Deanching with RplusMphoto

Cover artist: Michelle Sewell with RLS Images, Graphics and Designs.

[Edition Number] edition [Year of Publication]

SAMHSA'S (Substance Abuse and Mental Health Services Administration) National Helpline, 1-800-662-HELP (4357). (also known as the Treatment Referral Routing Service), or TTY: <u>1-800-487-4889</u> is a confidential, free 24-hour-a-day, 365-day a-year information service, in English and Spanish, for individuals and family members facing mental and/or substance use disorders. This service provides referrals to local treatment facilities, support groups, and community-based organizations.

Also visit the <u>online treatment locator</u> or send your zip code via text message: <u>435748</u> (HELP4U) to find help near you.

I have included this information as a way to hopefully reach out to those in need. My daughter is an addict, I pray for her every day that she will get help. She has lost many friends to suicide and overdose. If this helps anyone then it is worth it.

About the Author

Stephanie Webb Dillon resides in Memphis, Tennessee. She is married and has three daughters and six grandchildren. Stephanie enjoys spending time with her friends having game nights and crafting. Writing is her passion. She has completed her first book series this year and started two more. She is looking forward to traveling to book events in the next couple of years, meeting other authors, models, photographers and her readers.

You can follow her on her page at amazon.com/author/sdillon9614

Also By

Freedom Colorado Series:
Baked with Love
Playing for Keeps
Sheriff's Convenient Bride
Daddy's Second Chance
The Scars Within
Guarding her Heart

Men of Phoenix Security Series:
Hidden Desires
Uncovering her Secrets

Rippers MC Series:
Undertaker's Match
Christmas Boyfriend
Hawk's Redemption

1

Lillian- two weeks ago

I was sitting on the floor playing with Bethann and Hawk's boys when I heard the screeching of tires burning down the main drive of the compound. I got up to look out the window and saw the Medi-van going out of the gate followed by a couple of the guys in a truck. My stomach knotted up remembering them bringing Wolf home with a sheet over his body. If they had to take the van with them someone would have been seriously injured. I just prayed they could be saved. I watched the boys playing with their cars on the track and remembered being so excited about my baby. I was six months pregnant when Wolf went on his last job for the club. The Rippers' helped children who had been saved from trafficking to get adopted and start new lives. They also helped rescue them when they could. Wolf had gone on a rescue mission. They had found out about a house with several kids being held waiting to be sold. It was in Colorado Springs only about 100 miles from here. Wolf had become even more passionate about the cause since I got pregnant with our child. They managed to save four of the five kids being held but there was a shooting and Wolf took a bullet to his heart trying to shield a child from a bullet. They both died. They brought him home and then came to get me to take me to the morgue to say goodbye. I was so distraught that I had to be sedated. A week later I lost our baby.

Cameron tugged on my shirt, and I looked down at him. He wrinkled his nose and pointed to his brother. I chuckled as I started to smell the rank diaper.

"Ok buddy, I'll clean him up. Do you need to go to the potty?" I asked him and he squirmed. "Let's get you on the potty and I'll take care of Josh."

I picked Josh up and walked Cam into the bathroom. He pulled his pullup down and sat on his training potty. I grabbed a diaper and wipes from under the sink and laid Josh on a towel on the counter to change him. I heard the front door open as the alarm beeped and Bethann called out to me.

"We are in the bathroom." I called back as I put Josh back down on the floor and helped Cam clean up. "Good boy, Cameron. You will be in big boy undies in no time." He grinned at me then climbed on the stool to wash his hands. My little girl wouldn't be much older than him now. I felt the twinge in my heart at the thought of her. We came out of the hallway and Bethann scooped the boys up and hugged them. She put them at the table, and I saw they had some chicken tenders, mac and cheese along with some cut up fruit.

"Come sit down, we need to talk." Bethann said calmly. She came over and sat by me on the couch. "I don't know what your relationship is with Fury or if you even have one. I have seen the two of you interact and I know he has shown no interest in anyone but you, lately. Fury was taken by the Rippers' MC in Boston in retaliation to being outed trying to set up the Irish Mafia to take the fall for killing the head of the Italian mafia. Our guys stopped that from happening. They jumped

Fury and took him. When the Irish cleaned out the clubhouse, they found him badly beaten and tortured. They sent him back to us to recover. He is going to need a lot of care. I thought you should know."

I looked at Bethann in horror. I have been turning down Fury's advances for months. He has not been pushy, but he has been consistent and determined. It's not that I don't find him attractive. It's the opposite. I am too attracted to him. I swore after Wolf died that I would never fall for another biker. I stuck around because these guys were my family. They made me feel safe. Fury didn't bother me the first year after Wolf passed, but after that I started noticing that his eyes would track me across a room. I could feel his eyes on my body when I helped in the clubhouse. He sat at the counter many nights just talking to me and keeping me company. I realize now that he was slowly acclimating me to his presence. I have watched him plenty as well. He is a treat for the eyes at about six feet three inches of solid muscle, toned with a lick able six pack and ink that I had fantasized about tracing with my tongue. I was starting to cave and now he was injured.

"I don't know what you mean." I denied our connection to Bethann, I wasn't ready to talk about it. "I'm going to head home. I will see you later."

"He is going to be kept at Doc's place in one of the patient suites until he is able to get around on his own." Bethann told me as she went to check on the boys and clean up after their meal. "Call me if you need anything Lillian. Just remember, he is alive. You can't control who you fall in love with."

I got up, gathered my things and headed home. I looked around at the place I had called home for the last five years. Wolf and I had been very happy here together. The guys were like family to me, and I loved the women who had come to live here in the last year. Our house had three bedrooms because we wanted at least two children. I remember picking everything out and his joy in having it built for me. I stood in front of my home and looked at the wrap around porch and the swing as well as matching rockers on the other side of the door. I had planters on either side of the steps where I kept flowers during the warmer months. This place held a lot of good memories for me. I let myself inside and hung up my purse and coat. I looked through my freezer for something to eat and settled on a frozen pizza. After getting that in the oven I opened up a bottle of wine I had picked up at the grocery store last week. Pouring myself a glass I sat down at my bar and waited for my dinner to finish cooking.

After I finished eating, I took my wine and settled on the couch with a book. I didn't want the television on because I wanted to be able to hear when the guys got back. I wish I could say that I didn't care how Fury was but that wasn't true. I cared too much. He has been my rock and safe place over the last year and half. He stays quietly in the background most of the time. I just feel safe when he is in the room. I also feel hot and turned on when he turns those hazel eyes on me. The heat in those eyes makes me want things that I shouldn't. He is always so strong and fierce. He is known for being a skilled torturer, but he would never harm a woman or a child. He uses those skills on his enemies and anyone that threatens the club and its members. All the guys are very protective. I picked a book that I had already read previously because I know that I won't be able to focus fully on it. I just need a distraction for a while.

2

Hawk- two weeks ago

We pulled up to the airstrip and the plane was waiting for us. Doc backed up the van to the entrance of the plane. The door opened and a couple of Collum's men carried Fury down the stairs in a stretcher. They were being careful not to jostle him any more than necessary and I appreciated the care they showed my brother and best friend. He was in bad shape. I knew Doc would want to look at the chart and see his injuries for himself. He was frowning as they slid the stretcher beside the one that we had brought. After getting him transferred over and loaded, Doc climbed into the back with him, and Axle drove us back to the compound. It was a total head fuck seeing my friend in this shape. He was usually so strong and tough. He would hate looking weak. Doc gave him another sedative before we pulled out of the airfield to keep him as comfortable as possible for the drive.

"Damn, I wish I could bring my father back and kill him myself." I said as I followed behind the van with Rider on the passenger side. He grunted at me. I knew he felt the same. We felt sick about what had happened to Fury and wondered how they got him. I guess we wouldn't know until he wakes up and can tell us. The drive was long, and neither of us felt much like talking. We all had a hard time when we lost Wolf. He was such a great guy. Lillian had fallen apart. I noticed that she and Fury seemed to have developed a connection. I didn't know how far that went. Bethann said she would tell her about Fury when she got home. I'm glad I don't have to be the one to do that. When we pulled up outside Doc's place, he went in to make sure the room was ready then came out to help bring him in. We got him off the stretcher and settled. I stood back against the wall with my arms crossed while Doc set up an IV bag with fluids, antibiotics and pain meds. He was a great doctor and an irreplaceable asset to the club.

"I'm going to clean his wounds and redress them as I check him over. I would prefer limited visitors for the first twenty-four hours. Lillian is welcome to come see him and sit with him if she wants to." Doc told me as he continued to check Fury's wounds. I could see the frown on his face as he checked him over. "I know you guys are tight. I'll give you an update tomorrow. Go home to your family and rest. Right now, our biggest concern is infection."

"Okay, I'll be back tomorrow. Let me know if you need anything for him." I said before I turned to leave. I was ready to go home and put my arms around my girl.

I passed Lillian's place on my way home. I didn't stop because I didn't have any new information for her. She knows where Doc's place is if she wants to go check on him. I pulled up outside my place and parked the truck. I stared out the window for a minute and thought about how lucky I was. I just know that I don't ever want Beth to have to go through what Lillian went through a few years ago. I would be very diligent and careful. I wanted to always come home to her. I looked up and saw her standing at the door with a blanket wrapped around her shoulders. She didn't rush me, she just waited. I got out and went to her, pulling her into my arms. We went inside and cuddled on the couch. The boys were already asleep.

"I told Lillian what I could. She denies there is something going on, but I could tell she was upset." Beth said as she looked up at me.

"We will keep a check on her. This has to be bringing up memories of Wolf. It took months for her to talk to anyone after he passed, and she lost their baby." I told her, rubbing her back. All we can do is be there for them."

I sent a text to Lillian letting her know that we were back, and that Fury was at Doc's. I told her I would get her an update tomorrow. When I didn't hear back from her, I figured maybe she was asleep so went to bed.

The next morning, I went to check on Fury and walked in to find Lillian curled up in an armchair by the bed. She had a blanket wrapped around her and her arm tucked under her head. I didn't want to startle her, so I knocked on the door lightly. She blinked and looked up at me. I guess Doc put the blanket around her because she looked surprised to see it.

"Oh, I guess I fell asleep. I need to run home and shower so I can get to your house. What time is it?" she said standing up to stretch. Then she leaned over and kissed Fury on the cheek.

"It's about eight thirty, but it's Saturday so you don't need to worry about coming over. If you want to go shower, change and eat something I'll stay with him until you get back." I told her watching her slip on her coat and shoes. "Be careful walking back to your place."

"Thanks Hawk. I'll be back around lunch time. Let me know if anything changes." she said softly running her hand through her short black hair. With one more backward glance toward the bed she turned and left.

Doc walked in a few minutes after Lillian left and walked over to the bed to check Fury's bandages. He pulled them off, cleaned the wounds and redressed them. He looked pleased by what he saw.

"Looks good. No infection so far. We just have to be diligent about changing and cleaning the dressing until they close up. After a couple of days, I'll leave the dressing off and let them get some air." Doc stepped into the ensuite bathroom to wash his hands.

"Did she sit there all night?" I asked Doc as I nodded to the chair with the blanket folded in it. He nodded and frowned.

"I'm going to have to bring a cot in here or at least drag a recliner in if she insists on staying the night. I won't have her sleeping in a regular chair." He picked up the blanket and the chair, carrying it into his living area. "Hey Hawk come help me with this, so we don't make too much noise. I think she will take the recliner being in here better than a cot."

We moved the plush recliner into the corner of the room on the other side of Fury's bed. Since the IV and monitors were set up on the other side, we angled the chair where she could reach his hand if she wanted to.

"Are you going to be here for a while? I need to run to the hospital and check on a few patients." Doc asked. "I'd rather not leave him alone right now."

"Yeah, I told Lillian I'd stay with him until she got back. She went home to shower, change and eat." I told him as I sat down and got comfortable. "Go do what you need to do. We won't leave him."

Doc just nodded and left. I sat and checked emails on my phone and messaged my friend Collum to see if they had come across any members unaccounted for. So far nothing. I just know that the chances that every member of the club was there that night are very slim. I didn't want anyone coming here to start trouble.

3

*L*illian

    I had not planned to go to Doc's last night, but I could not sleep. My thoughts had stayed with the gruff, sexy bald man that was across the lot unconscious. I could not stop thinking the worst and I needed to see him for myself. I had got dressed, put on my coat and boots and walked over to Doc's place. When I went in the room and saw him laying there motionless and looking pale as death it squeezed my heart. I pulled the chair closer to his bed and sat down. I curled up in the chair and laid my head on my arm and reached out with the other to hold his hand. I just needed to be touching him to know he was still warm and alive.

    I must have fallen asleep like that because when Hawk came in, I was covered in a blanket. I guess Doc came in sometime in the night to check on Fury and covered me up. My neck was stiff so I stripped down and started the shower, getting in with it as hot as I could stand it and letting it pelt my neck to loosen up the knots. Washing my hair and my body before getting out to dry off. I ran a little leave in conditioner in my hair and then got dressed. Picking some warm leggings and a long sweater. I decided to grab a few things to take back with me since I knew I was going to be there for a while. Throwing some books and my e-reader in a bag along with some snacks. I fixed myself a sandwich and sat down to eat. I was just finishing up when my phone rang.

I answered the phone and before I could say anything I could hear Fury in the background calling for me. He sounded distraught.

"I need you to come back. I can't get him to calm down and he is going to rip his stitches." Hawk said.

"I'm on my way." I hung up, put on my coat, grabbed my bag and ran back over to Doc's. I walked into the room and went straight to Fury. He was thrashing and calling my name. I took his hand in mine and started to talk to him calmly. As soon as he registered my voice he started to calm down and stopped moving. I could see blood under the sheet where it looked like he had ripped open his stitches.

"Well shit, looks like I'm going to have to call Doc to stitch him back up." Hawk swore under his breath. He grabbed some gauze out of the bathroom cabinet and put it on the wound holding it. "Here is my phone, shoot Doc a message 911 and let him know that Fury needs to be stitched back up."

My hands shaking, I took his phone and sent the message. A few minutes later it beeped in my hand. Doc was on his way back. I put Hawk's phone on the tray table and went to get a damp wash cloth and some antiseptic wipes. I put them down by the bed along with a suture kit that I found in one of the drawers and some extra gauze and scissors. Then I went looking for some clean bedding. I heard him start to call me again and ran back into the room.

"I guess someone else will have to get clean sheets. I'm going to sit here and hold his hand to keep him calm." I said gently rubbing Fury's hand against my cheek. I murmured soothing nonsense to him, and he settled again. "Looks like I'm staying." Hawk grunted as he held the area where the stitches were torn. Doc walked in cursing when he saw the blood.

"Well, damnit I was hoping not to have to redo stitches." Doc started to go in search of supplies when he saw them all on the tray. He looked up at me and smiled. "You did this?"

"Yes, before he started thrashing and calling out for me again. Looks like you have an additional house guest for a while." I told him as I sat back in the chair and continued to hold Fury's hand. As long as he was touching me or could hear me, he stayed calm.

"As long as it keeps him calm, I'm fine with that. You're going to need more than what you brought." He said while he cleaned the wound and removed the torn stitches, replacing them with fresh ones and then fresh bandages.

"I can give Hawk my key with a list and Bethann can get what I need from my house." I said watching as he cleaned up the used supplies. I took the damp cloth I had brought in and wiped the sweat from Fury's forehead and face where he broke into a sweat during his panic. I gently rubbed my hand along the top of his head in a soothing motion. He frowned in his sleep, clearly in pain. Doc put a shot of morphine into his IV to help ease the pain and help him get more rest.

"I don't know why he wants me here, but I'll be here for him as long as he needs me. He does so much for everyone else and is always doing the club's dirty work. He deserves to be taken care of for a change." I know I sounded resentful; I couldn't help it. He is always the one they call for the unpleasant jobs that had to be done. "If you will hand me my phone, I'll call Bethann and tell her what I need. Hawk, my keys are in the side pocket in my purse. You may have to see if Annie can watch the boys next week, at least until he wakes up."

"We will take care of it. I have plenty of coverage at Trixie's. I can watch my boys for Bethann to work and for you to take care of our boy here." Hawk said as he handed me my phone. I shot her a quick text telling her what I needed and then put my phone down on the table. I looked at him and felt bad. Fury was his best friend; they were as close as brothers. I know it was killing him to see Fury in this condition.

"It's not your fault, you know. He wouldn't want you to blame yourself." I told him as he headed out the door. "I have a duffle bag in the hall closet she can put the stuff in."

"I'll drop it by a little later along with dinner. Any requests." He asked. I looked down at my hand holding Fury's and smiled.

"Something I can eat with one hand would be good." I tried to smile at him. He nodded with a grunt and left. Doc had gone to get a clean set of sheets. Axle followed him into the room.

"I'm here to check on him and help Doc put clean sheets on the bed. Do you want to leave the room?" Axle asked me, but Doc emphatically shook his head no.

"Are you insane? Her leaving is why we are changing the sheets. He went berserk when she left earlier. It took her touching and talking to him to settle him down. She stays." Doc said firmly. I smiled up at Axle and shrugged my shoulders.

"Ok then, we will have to turn him towards you first to undo the sheet and then move him toward the other side to remove it. We are going to do this carefully. You may have to let go for a minute. Just talk to him when you do." Doc instructed as they set about changing his bedding. When everything was done, we covered him back up and they left us alone. I reached into my bag and grabbed my water bottle and a pack of crackers to snack on so my blood sugar wouldn't drop. I was really tired so I put the recliner back, covered up with the blanket and turned towards the bed so I could have my hand on his arm. In a soft voice I sang to him before falling asleep.

4

Fury – one week ago

My head was pounding, everything hurt. I had flashes of someone knocking me over the head and then waking up in a dank basement tied to a chair and being beaten and tortured. They didn't want information, they just wanted to hurt me. They succeeded. I also had flashes of a soft hand touching my forehead and holding my hand. A husky feminine voice talking to me while I slept. I knew that voice. I tried to open my eyes. The light hurt but at least the pain let me know I was alive. I don't remember how I got out, just vague memories of being loaded on a plane and then not much else. I finally forced my eyes open and turned my head slightly to where I felt the weight on my hand. I saw midnight black hair curling around her ears, pale skin connected to the hand holding onto mine. Lillian was here. I have been trying for months to get her to go out with me. She wouldn't budge, now she was here holding vigil while I'm stuck in a bed too weak to do anything. I tried to speak but my mouth was so dry all I could do was gasp. It must have been enough to wake her up because she raised her head and looked at me with those gorgeous blue eyes.

"Oh Fury, you're awake. We have been so worried." she said softly. I tried to lick my lips, but I had no moisture. "You must be so thirsty. Let me get you some water and get Doc to check on you."

I watched her walk out of the room and then a few minutes later she came back with some water in a cup with a straw for me. Following behind her was Doc.

"Well, did you have a good nap?" Doc asked in his usual smart-ass tone. "You have had us all worried. Sleeping for a week. I flipped him off and took a sip of the water that Lillian held to my lips. After a few sips I felt like I could speak.

"How did you find me?" I asked, wishing I could remember more. "I don't remember much more than being hit over the head and then waking up to a beating."

"The Irish took out the club in Boston. They found you in the basement in bad shape. Hawk's friend Collum got you out and on a plane home. He called us to pick you up at the airfield." Doc said as he ran a hand through his wavy hair. The man looked exhausted. "You have been here for a week. You came to us with three busted ribs, massive bruising, your face beaten to shit, your eyes were swollen shut, left leg broken. I wrapped your ribs and set your leg. I have been treating your wounds that Collum had stitched before sending you home. You are on the mend, but it will be a while before you can do much on your own. You are looking at five to six weeks for your ribs and your leg to heal. It's better for you to stay here for the next couple weeks, then you can move back to your room in the clubhouse with help."

"I need to go home and shower before I head over to watch Cameron and Josh. Call me if you need something. I can bring it when Bethann gets home from work." Lillian said as she slipped on her coat and picked up her keys. She looked at me for a minute, then turned and left. I watched her leave wondering why she was even here.

I looked up at Doc with a confused look on my face. He shook his head.

"You were inconsolable the first time you showed any sign of consciousness. You were calling for her. We couldn't calm you down until she showed up and took your hand. She started talking to you and you settled." Doc told me. "She has been here every day and stayed by your bedside except to use the bathroom and shower, she even has her meals here."

I knew she looked tired, but I had no idea she had been sleeping in my room every night. If I find out they haven't been making sure she eats, I'll be kicking ass as soon as I am able.

"I'm insulted, of course I have made sure she was fed. I have been bringing her meals. I cook or order dinner for us here. She tried going home the first night, but you started to thrash again until she took your hand. She has been here since." Doc rubbed his face. "Are you hungry?"

"I'm starving. I could eat a horse." I told him as my stomach growled. He chuckled at me.

"You haven't had solid food in over a week. We will start you with broth first." Doc went to the kitchen to get some food. I figured I needed the bathroom then realized I had a catheter and groaned. Like that wasn't emasculating in front of a beautiful woman. I closed my eyes but tried not to fall back asleep until I got something on my stomach.

Doc came back in with a large mug of broth. He raised the bed up so I could drink it. It was the best tasting broth I had ever had. Probably because I was so hungry. I tried to finish it but found I was full. Huh, guess my stomach shrunk from not eating in over a week.

I really wanted to ask questions about my captivity and how they got me out, but I felt myself starting to doze off.

5

Lillian – present day

It was almost February, and I was trying to decide how I wanted to spend my Saturday. Fury was doing better, although he still had a lot of healing to do before he could be on his own again. I had been spending all my spare time at Doc's helping to take care of him. Last night when he snapped my head off for no good reason, I decided I have had enough. I am going to go get groceries, some wine and stay in today. I would catch up on my laundry and then relax with a good book. No grouchy biker for me today.

Pouring myself a cup of coffee, I sat down to read the paper. Nothing interesting really happens around here. I opened the blinds in my picture window when I came in so I could see the snow falling outside. Luckily my job was within walking distance. If I was going to the store I needed to get dressed and head out. while the streets were salted and plowed, it was still dangerous to drive when the snow started coming down harder. We were supposed to have blizzard conditions this week. I finished my coffee then put on my jeans, a warm turtleneck sweater and my boots. Putting my purse on my shoulder, I got in my car to head into town. I waved at one of the new prospects watching the gate and drove to the main grocery store in town.

I looked around as I was driving, and it was like living in a snow globe. The town was fairly small, and the main street was charming with small businesses owned by residents here in Liberty. There was the Diner that everyone ate at all the time, the flower shop 'Coming up Roses', a salon 'Cuttin' Up'. There were more but I just loved living here. I pulled into a free parking spot in front of the store and got out. As I walked in, I saw Sophie and Annie in line to pay. I walked over to greet them.

"Hey ladies. I can't believe your guys let you out on your own to shop." I commented knowing how protective Undertaker and Gears both are.

"They didn't, Gears is waiting in the car keeping it warm. We rode together, Zeke is watching Mattie." Annie said smirking. "That was his compromise, I could ride with Gears and Sophie. Of course, I jumped at the chance to get out of the house for a little bit before the worst of the weather hits."

"Yeah, I figured I better stock up while I had the chance." I said as I took a basket. "I'll catch up with you girls, later." They waved at me, and I went to gather what I needed. Since I lived alone, my supplies lasted a lot longer. I made sure to grab some staple items that could be eaten if we lost power. Although the clubhouse had a generator and we all gathered there for meals if that happened. I just wanted to be prepared so I could stay in my house if I wanted to. When I finished with the grocery part, I walked over to the wine section and selected a few bottles of my favorite red Moscato. Always good to have on hand. I turned the corner and almost ran into a petite brunette. She looked up at me and blushed.

"Oh Lillian, please don't tell Fang I'm in town." Katherine, Fang's sister, was just out of university. She was supposed to be starting an internship at some point.

"He doesn't know you're in town, why for heaven's sake?" I was surprised. I knew that Fang adored his baby sister. She was a surprise and quite a bit younger than our silver fox biker. He doted on her. "It will break his heart if he finds out you're in town and didn't call him."

"You know how overprotective they all are. I want a little freedom. He would expect me to move back into the house on the property. I'm not ready for that. I want to spread my wings a little." Katherine said as she put a couple of bottles of wine in her cart.

"If you're working at Liberty Memorial he is going to find out, because Doc works a rotation in the ER." I told her raising an eyebrow. "You really should just tell him you're back and that you have your own place already."

"I know you're right, just give me a few days to get settled in first." Katherine said pleading with me. I nodded and gave her a hug.

"Ok, but once you tell him I expect you to come over for wine and gossip one night." I winked at her and headed to the register to check out.

Standing in line, my phone beeped with a text. I looked at it and it was Fury wanting to know where I was and why I wasn't at Doc's. I scoffed and put my phone on silent. The nerve of that man, after snapping my head off last night to expect me to just come back over for more abuse. I checked out, loaded my groceries in the car and headed back to my house. After the third time the phone vibrated, I reached over and just turned the damn thing off. When I pulled up to my house, I saw Axle standing outside waiting for me. What the hell?

I pulled into my garage and popped my trunk so I could take my groceries in. I was not in the mood for an inquisition.

"Why aren't you answering your phone, Lillian? Fury was freaking out thinking something had happened to you." Axle said in his president tone. I took a few bags and started to walk inside.

"If you are going to stand there, grab a few bags and help." I hollered out to him as I went into my kitchen to put the bags on the counter. He followed a minute later with most of the rest of them. I turned to him with my arms crossed over my chest. "I don't owe Fury an explanation of where I go and when. I didn't answer the phone because I don't want to speak to him right now."

"You know he has been through a lot the last few weeks and he is going crazy in that bed not able to do anything." Axle reminded me.

"I am well aware of that Axle. Who the hell do you think has been by his bedside the last few weeks taking care of him and watching over him. I'll tell you. ME!!! And what do I get in return? I get him snapping my head off for trying to help his sorry ass to the bathroom. So, fuck him and fuck you. I just want some peace for the day. Is that too much to ask?"

I stomped back out to my car to grab the last couple of bags and close my trunk. I walked past him and started putting up my groceries. Axle was frowning at me.

"I'm sure he didn't mean it and he probably wants to apologize for being an ass. He can't exactly walk or drive over here to do it. So could you cut us a break and go see him. If not at least call him back." Axle pleaded with me. I took a deep breath, closed my eyes and nodded my head.

"Fine, but first I'd like to put my groceries up." I put a bottle of the wine in the fridge and the other bottles in my rack. I already knew I would be opening a bottle tonight. "You need a woman, someone to focus on besides me."

"You know I'm not the settling down type. Besides I have plenty to keep me busy around here." He smiled at me, eyes twinkling with mischief. He was a handsome bastard, the girls lined up to get a piece of him. He was like a brother to me though. "Just try to cut him a little slack. You know he is not the kind to sit still so he is going crazy and the better he feels the worse it will be until he is healed and can get back to normal."

"I'll try, but I will not let him run over me. Now get out of here I'm sure you have better things to do then pester me." I said as he hugged me tweaked my nose. Ugh just like a big brother I never knew I wanted.

"Be careful Lil, let me know if you need anything." he said as he headed back out the door. I finished putting away my groceries and went to start a load of laundry. Sitting down at my table I pulled my phone out and turned it back on. I dialed and waited.

"Lily, where have you been?" Fury answered in his raspy voice. I closed my eyes as I felt his voice all through my body. "I've been waiting for you."

"Waiting for what Fury, you made it clear last night that you didn't need me or want me there." I told him remembering the hurt and anger I felt last night when He told me he didn't need my help and to go home. So that's what I did. It's the first night since they brought him back that I haven't spent by his bedside. "I'm staying home today. I don't need to be somewhere I'm not wanted."

I heard him sigh and I could just picture him running his hand over his handsome face. I was about to hang up when he started talking again.

"Baby, I'm sorry. I was in pain, frustrated and I hate looking weak in front of you. It's hard on a man's ego, ya know?" he said softly. "Please come back over."

"I have some things I need to do here. I'll try to come back over for dinner." I told him knowing I was getting too attached to this man.

"Thank you, Lily." Fury sounded so tired. "I'm sorry that I was rude to you last night. I really didn't mean it."

"You're forgiven, now let me finish my chores and I'll see you later." I told him as I hung up. I put my phone down and thought back to before his accident. He had been a daily part of my life over the last year and half. Always hanging at the clubhouse when I was there helping. He took his dinner in the kitchen with me. I haven't seen him take a woman to his room there in well over six months. I knew back when I was with Wolf that Fury would have no problem sprawling on the couch and letting one of the club whores suck him off or bending one over the pool table. About a year after Wolf passed, he started taking them to his room instead of taking them in the common area, then sometime over the summer I noticed that he wasn't hanging around any of them. They still came on to him, but he turned them down. I had heard from a couple of the guys that he would lock himself in his room during the parties they had. He started asking me out a few months ago. I have not accepted yet. I was about to give in to a date when he was taken. Now I was scared to get too close to him for fear of losing him too. I pulled my clothes out of the dryer and started to put them away. Looking at the clock I see it's about four in the afternoon. I knew Doc made sure he ate so I fixed myself a sandwich to eat before I went to see him.

6

Fury

After I spoke with Lillian I felt better. I had been an ass last night and she had every reason to be pissed at me. She has been here watching over me for the last few weeks. I let my aggravation at feeling helpless get the better of me last night and I lashed out at her. Ugh, I'm lucky she is a forgiving person. I heard a noise and looked up to see Axle, Hawk and Rider come into my room.

"Hey Fury, how are you feeling?" Hawk asked me. "Looks like you could use a shave."

"I'm here, tired of being stuck in this damn bed." I grumbled at them. "Is someone finally going to tell me what happened?"

"That's one of the reasons were here. Doc says you've been asking about it." Axle said as he pulled up a chair and sat down. "So, from what you've told Doc, all you remember is being hit in the head and then waking up in their torture basement."

"Yeah, that's right. Bastards are going to pay when I get better." I said with malice in my voice. I saw them look at each other and I didn't like the looks they were giving off. "What aren't you telling me?"

"Collum O'Leary, head of the Irish Mafia found you. They were going after my father who tried to set them up and when they rolled up in the clubhouse it was a mess. They took out the entire club. Found you in the basement being worked over by my dad and one of his buddies. They managed to find out who you were with, before they finished them off. Collum was responsible for saving you and getting you back home." Hawk told me looking me in the eye. He knew I would be fried that I wouldn't have anyone to go after.

"Yeah, they didn't want anything other than to make me hurt and use me to lash out at our chapter here." Fury hissed. "Snake took great joy in telling me that they had sent my cut to you and taunted you with the fact that they took me."

"I won't say I'm sorry they are all gone because I'm not. That chapter was toxic and gave our club a bad name. They burned the clubhouse to the ground. I told them we would not be rebuilding there." Axle said looking me in the eye. "Guys, you want to give us a minute. I need to have a quick chat with Fury about another matter."

Shit, I knew he was going to lay into me about Lillian. I'm glad I already called and apologized to her. We don't disrespect our women and I should never have spoken to her like I did. I watched Hawk and Rider leave the room and close the door behind them. Axle turned back to me, and I knew.

"You know I had my reservations about you pursuing a relationship with Lillian. I know what you have been like with women in the past. She has struggled to put her life back together. That being said, I have noticed you seem to have given up your man whoring ways. Whatever you said to her last night I hope you have apologized for it. She was pissed and ready to write you off." He said to me rubbing his chin.

"She called me back earlier and I apologized. She said she would be over in a while. I know I screwed up and I can't promise it won't happen again, but I will do my best." I said as I looked up and saw her in the doorway. She was wearing some fitted black jeans and a long pale blue sweater that matched her eyes. Her hair curling around her ears. "Come on in Lily, I'm sure Axle was just leaving."

Axle chuckled and got up offering her the chair. She smiled at him and sat down. "I'll talk to you later. Holler if you need anything."

I jerked my head at him as he went out the door, then I focused on the beauty sitting beside me. She looked at me and touched my beard. I haven't been able to shave since I got back, and she isn't used to seeing me like this. Well except for the last two weeks.

"What do you think of the beard? Should I keep it?" I teased her. She wrinkled her nose and shook her head.

"I like being able to see those dimples. Although maybe it's safer for me if I don't." she blushed while biting her lip. I wanted to bite that lip myself. I wanted to kiss her so badly.

"You like my dimples huh? You saying they help get me out of trouble?" I winked at her, and she giggled. Wow, that was a great sound. I felt that in my cock, and I would make it my goal to hear it more. "You should laugh more."

"I haven't had a lot of reasons to laugh in the last few years." She whispered. I noticed she was wringing her hands. I reached down to lace my fingers with hers. I missed that. She did that a lot while I was in and out of consciousness. It's one constant I can remember. "How are you feeling?" she asked me while staring at my lips. I groaned wanting her to lean closer.

"I'm okay. I just hate that all this happened, and I still haven't got to take you on a date yet." I teased, rubbing my thumb along her knuckles. I felt goosebumps form on her and noticed her nipples harden and her breath quicken. Good, she is attracted to me.

"Well, maybe when you are back on your feet you can remedy that." she said boldly. Lillian stood up and walked over to the door. I was worried she was going to leave, and I didn't want to be alone with my thoughts.

"Don't leave yet?" I asked her. She looked back at me and smiled.

"I'm not leaving, I was going to find out when Doc planned to bring your dinner. Are you getting hungry?" she asked me.

"No, I'm not hungry right now. Would you help me shave this off?" I asked rubbing the beard that had grown the last couple of weeks. It was itchy and I wanted it gone. Her eyes flicked over my face and stayed on mine. She moved away from the door.

"Let me check the bathroom for supplies, I'll be right back." She walked into the ensuite bathroom to look for a razor and some shaving cream. A few minutes later she came back in with a disposable cup of hot water, a towel, shaving cream and a razor. "I'm going to go grab some scissors, I'll be right back."

I looked at the supplies she placed on the tray table and wondered if she had ever done this before. She walked back in with a pair of scissors in her hand and went about putting the towel under my chin and started to clip at the excess hair until she had it close to my face. Taking that towel to the window, she raised it and dumped the hair outside shaking it off. I watched as she closed the window back and went to get a clean towel and washcloth. She placed the warm washcloth over my mouth and neck. She let it sit for a few minutes before removing it and putting shaving cream on my mustache and beard.

"Tilt your head back for me. I'm going to start with your mustache." she said softly. I watched her as she focused on what she was doing. She made steady even strokes and then wiped off the excess cream before moving to my neck. She took her time, cleaning the razor between swipes. When she was finished, she went and dumped the cup in the bathroom coming back out with the washcloth warmed up and used it to wipe my face. I watched her take the supplies to the bathroom and she brought me a hand mirror. Holding it up for my inspection.

I looked at it and rubbed my hand over it. I felt so much better, I should have asked her to shave my head as well. I handed the mirror back to her and she put it away before coming back to sit down.

"Thank you, Lily. Maybe if you feel like it tomorrow you could shave my head as well." I asked her hopefully. She nodded and started to say something when Doc came into the room with a tray of food.

"Hey, you're looking more like yourself today. Good job Lily." Doc said smiling at us. "I brought you a steak, baked potato and some asparagus. There is enough for you both. There is also some tea there for the both of you as well. I'm going to head into town for a shift at the ER. If she leaves, be sure to call one of the guys if you need to try and get up."

"Thanks Doc." We said at the same time, then laughed. "I'm staying the night. I'll take care of grumpy bear here."

"Hey, I'm not grumpy today." I said in mock hurt. Then I winked at her. "Get out of here Doc, I want time alone with my girl."

I heard Doc laughing as he left, closing the door behind him. Lily arranged the tray so that we could both reach the food. She cut up my steak since my left hand was still healing from where they had cut me up. Doc was supposed to take the stiches out in a couple of days. I couldn't wait.

"This looks delicious. That man will make someone a great husband one day, as long as she can deal with the hours he works." She said as she took a bite and moaned. My cock kicked in my pants, and I closed my eyes trying to get control over my body. She licked her lips and I groaned.

"Are you okay, are you hurting anywhere?" she asked concerned. I shook my head.

"Baby, nothing hurts except my pride. Those noises you're making are killing me. I would love to be able to lay you down and make love to you all night long and we haven't even kissed yet." I told her watching the blush steal across her cheeks. "Just eat your dinner, Lily."

We ate in silence and just enjoyed the companionship. I liked that she enjoyed her food and didn't eat like a rabbit. She was perfect and I wouldn't change a thing about her. When we finished, she took the dishes to the kitchen and rinsed them off putting them in the dishwasher. As she came back into the room, she walked over to the side of the bed and leaned over me. She stopped when she got close to my mouth and looked me in the eyes as she pressed her lips to mine. I put my hand to the back of her head and held her there while I explored her mouth with my tongue and deepened the kiss. She tasted like the steak we had eaten and something unique to her. I eased up my grip on her head and she slowly pulled back and looked at me.

"That was nice." She said and did it again. This time when she raised her head up, she stepped back. "I've wondered what it would be like to kiss you."

"I have wondered about kissing you as well." I told her. "Why don't you climb up here beside me and we can watch a movie. That way we will both be comfortable. It's not like I'm in any shape to take advantage of you yet."

She giggled again and kicked off her shoes. I slowly eased over a little to offer her some room. She climbed on my side where my ribs weren't bruised or broken. I pulled the blanket over us both and we flipped the television on a movie channel. I let her choose and to my surprise she chose one of the new Star Trek movies to watch. Who knew my girl was a closet geek. I had my arm around her and her head on my shoulder. I guess this could be considered a first date. Not one I would have planned but I wasn't complaining.

7

Lillian

The last few weeks went by quickly. Fury was healing up well. All his stitches had been removed, his ribs no longer taped, and he was given weights to start building his strength back up. We went for slow walks around the house at first and then around the property. When I wasn't watching Cameron and Josh I was with Fury. Doc said he was cleared to go back to the clubhouse as long as he didn't try to overdo it.

He has been at my house more than his room the last past week. I have really enjoyed having him there. He helps with the cooking, and we cuddle while watching tv. He holds me at night while we sleep too. We haven't had sex yet; we are waiting for him to cleared for regular activity. The guys all have a job coming up and he really wants to be a part of it. I know he misses working and while I worry, I won't be the woman that begs him to stay home. That's not who he is. I have been an old lady and I know the drill. We are still seeing where things take us at this point. If he gets the 'all clear' from Doc, we are supposed to go out for dinner after to celebrate and I'm hoping we come back home and do more celebrating. I am so horny I feel like I am wet all the time. We have done some heavy petting, but that's it.

I'm curled up on the couch at Hawk and Bethann's reading a book while the boy's nap. It's about two in the afternoon so they will be up soon, and Bethann will be home before I know it. I wanted to help her out, so I started a pot of chicken and dumplings this morning in her crockpot. I have one going at my house as well. It's a nice winter comfort meal and I enjoy leftovers. Fury is at his appointment and then he is going to workout with a couple of the guys. I think he also plans to go to the range to get in some practice. It's been a long two months for him. Axle made him wait a full eight weeks to get back into the field and only with Doc's approval. He wanted to know he was back at one hundred percent. They don't take unnecessary chances. It's one of the only reasons I'm willing to date him. Losing Wolf was hard, and I already feel strongly about Fury. I couldn't bear to lose him too.

I hear Josh talking and get up to go check on the boys. Since he started trying to climb out of his crib, Hawk put it to the toddler bed setting. That way he can get down without hurting himself. Cameron finally finished potty training, so he is in big boy pants. I just have to remind him sometimes to go. He gets up and goes to the bathroom and Josh follows him. When he is finished, Josh wants to try. It's really cute how he tries to mimic his brothers' actions. I sit him down on the training potty and show him how to point his little penis into the toilet as to not make a mess. When he goes, he gets so excited. I pull his pullup back on him and help him wash his hands, then take him to the kitchen for a reward. The boys like yogurt pouches so I gave him one of those. It's a healthy snack and a treat at the same time. I put one of their shows on and checked on dinner. I put the crockpot on warm and read a story to the boys while we wait for their mom to get home.

I think it's so sweet that they adopted them. Seeing Hawk as a father is so cute. I wonder what Fury would be like as one. I quickly tried to clear that thought from my head. I was reading when Bethann came in along with Hawk right behind her. They were smiling and laughing with each other. Cameron spotted them and ran over to Hawk, who scooped him up into his arms for a hug. Josh followed and went to him as well.

"I guess I'm chopped liver." Bethann laughed watching them. Hawk just winked at her. "Something smells good, Lillian you didn't have to cook."

"It's cold outside and I thought a pot of dumplings would make a nice meal for you guys. I have the same thing in my crockpot at home for tonight." I told them smiling when Cameron wanted down and came to hug me goodbye. "It's ready whenever you are. I'm going to head on home."

"Fury was headed that way when I came in, so he is probably waiting for you at your place." Hawk gave me a knowing look. "I hear he got an all clear from Doc."

"That's great. I'll see you two tomorrow." I said as I put on my coat and picked up my purse to go. I walked to my house as quickly as I could. I couldn't wait to see him. As I walked up to the door, Fury opened it and pulled me inside locking the door behind us. I hung up my purse and coat and then suddenly I was backed against the door with his body pressed into mine.

"You have been driving me crazy for over a year. I feel like I'm going to explode with wanting you." He growled in my face before he took my mouth in a searing kiss. He used his body to hold me against the door and cupped my face in his large hands as he plundered my mouth. I whimpered and put my arms around his torso to feel him even closer. He started to kiss his way down my neck, but I had on a sweater. He leaned back and pulled the sweater off. Then looked at my breasts in the lacy bra I was wearing and licked his lips. He leaned down and sucked on my breast through the lace, dragging a moan from me. He reached up and unclasped the bra releasing my breasts from their confines. He went back to sucking and licking them both alternating between them. I grabbed his shirt to pull over his head and he moved back long enough to pull it off for me, then went back to what he was doing. I had my eyes closed, focusing on the pleasure of this man's mouth on my body when it stopped. I opened my eyes to look at him. He was staring at me reverently.

"What is your real name?" I asked him, realizing that I didn't know. He smiled up at me.

"It's Brian Nash. You can call me Brian if you want." He whispered as he stood in front of me and pulled me toward the bedroom. I followed him eagerly, dragging my pants off along the way. When we got to my bed, he had stripped off the rest of his clothing as well. I stared at his body, it was like a work of art. All the muscled ridges and artwork decorating it. I licked my lips and crooked my finger at him.

"I need to touch you." I told him, suddenly wanting to put my mouth on every part of his body. He walked over to me and pushed me back onto the bed. Then he grabbed my legs and pulled me to the edge of the bed dropping to his knees in front of me.

"Next time, right now if you touch me this is going to be over before I really get started." He placed his mouth on me and licked me from top to bottom and back again. He feasted on me like a starving man and all I could do was watch and writhe in pleasure. He dipped his tongue in my channel and tongue fucked me for a minute before adding fingers to the mix and working my clit with his tongue until I flew apart. I looked down to see him sucking my juices off his fingers and licking his lips before raising up and wrapping my legs around his waist. He lined himself up with my entrance leaning over me and then thrust into my body in one stroke. I knew there was something we were forgetting but my mind was mush. I touched his chest and slid my arms around him to pull him closer. He used his hands on my ass to angle me for deeper penetration and then fucked me hard.

"I want you to come again baby. Can you do that for me?" he grunted as he changed the angle with one of my legs up by his neck and me partially on my side. Suddenly he was rubbing my g-spot, and I erupted all over him pulsing around his cock as his eyes rolled back and he came. Gently he put my leg down and pulled out. "Stay here." I watched his magnificent ass walk to the bathroom. I heard running water and then he was back with a damp cloth to clean me up. After putting the washcloth in the bathroom, he pulled back the covers and we climbed under them. Fury pulled me against his chest.

"Starting to wish I had said yes to a date months ago. That was amazing." I whispered. I felt him chuckle. I was thinking about starting round two when my stomach let out a very unladylike growl.

"I think I need to feed my girl. How do you feel about pizza?" Fury asked me as his stomach started to growl too. "We need fuel for the rest of the night." He reached over and grabbed his phone and placed an order then laid it back down on the nightstand and pulled me close. I laid there beside him tracing the tattoos on his chest with my finger. I started to trace them lower when he stopped me. I looked up at him and saw the hunger on his face.

"Baby, I need to throw on some pants so I can get our pizza. It's paid for but I don't want one of the guys to see what's mine when they bring it up to the house." He said firmly as he leaned over to press a kiss to my lips before slipping out of the bed. I watched him as he pulled on a pair of jeans leaving the button undone. "Why don't you throw on my shirt and some leggings and come into the living room with me. I'll get a fire going in the fireplace while we wait for our dinner."

I climbed out of the bed, snatched up my leggings along with his shirt and went to the bathroom. After taking care of business and getting dressed I joined him in the living room. When I walked in, I saw he had the fire going.

"Whatcha doing?" I asked him as I watched him putter around my kitchen. I thought seeing another man in my space that I shared with Wolf would make me uncomfortable but seeing Fury here just felt right.

"I'm just fixing us something to drink and gathering a couple of plates. The app said the driver is on his way with our food. I'm sorry, I didn't realize you had cooked." He said as he put the plates and drinks on the table then came over to sit by me on the couch.

"It's fine, the dumplings can go in the fridge for tomorrow night." I curled up beside him while we waited. Fury wasn't a chatty sort. He wasn't big on meaningless conversation, and I wasn't either. We could enjoy each other's company without feeling the need to fill the time talking. I turned the television to a news station so we could get updated on the weather. After our pizza arrived, we moved to the table to eat. When we finished, I put away our leftovers and put the dumplings in the fridge for the next night. I was going to turn off the tv when I saw Fury freeze up and I looked at the screen to see a photo of a rough looking biker. They were looking for him in connection with an arson case as well as murder. I looked back at Fury to see him still sitting there not moving. I walked around the couch to kneel in front of him.

"Fury?" I said his name softly and he didn't respond. His eyes glued to the television. "Brian, baby look at me?" I put my hands on either side of his face stroking his cheeks gently. He blinked, looking down at me suddenly and then back at the television. I glanced back and the picture was gone.

"I need to talk to Axle and Hawk. I'll be right back baby." He said as I watched him button his jeans and throw on a hoodie and his boots. I frowned as I watched him leave. I really didn't like the look on his face. I had a bad feeling about this. With a sigh, I grabbed a blanket off the back of the couch and wrapped it around me. I knew he was going to be a while.

8

Fury

    I was taken back when I saw that man's face on the tv screen. I knew it was too much to hope for that all of the club in Boston had been irradicated. Viper was one of the guys who had helped torture me. He must have been out on an errand when everything went down. It made me wonder how many they missed. We needed to get our hands on him so we could find out. I hated seeing the fear on Lillian's face when she realized that I recognized him. I don't want to lose her now that we are finally a couple. I pulled open the door to the clubhouse and saw the guys all at the large table we used for meetings and meals. I walked over and sat down.

    "Viper is still alive and on the loose. That means there could be a few others as well. He usually traveled with his buddy Razor. It's likely the two of them were out whoring when everything went down. I was in and out of consciousness, but I tried to listen to everything that was said in my presence. They didn't care about talking in front of me because they planned to kill me." I told the guys who made noises of discontent.

"What station was it on?" Gears asked me. "I can pull up the recording and send a picture to all of our phones." He was already on his laptop typing something into it.

"Channel three, national news. Apparently, he offed one of Collum's family. A well-known restaurant owner in Southie." I told them, rubbing my chin as I thought about it.

"Damn, I liked Connor O'Leary. He was a good guy. Collum will be out for blood." Hawk said with a scowl. "Connor never was a part of the family business, but everyone knew he was family because Collum had his meetings at his place and all his guys liked to eat there."

"We have a job in Oregon going down in a couple of days. We will have to split up to handle both." Axle said as he did the math. "I really don't want to leave us short, but I also don't know if they realize that Fury didn't die in that fire. We can't leave the women and families here unprotected."

"What if Gears stays behind with Undertaker? When you get back, we go hunting." I suggested. "I suggest we also have the women and children stay at the clubhouse together so that it's easier to watch all of them."

"That's fine, Sophie and Bethann can work from their laptops as well as I can. Lillian and Annie can take care of the boys. The shop will be closed until we get back. We will make this work." Gears said. Everyone voiced their agreement.

"Ok, so we will leave in two days. Make sure everyone is ready. I'll have extra prospects on the gate." Axle said. "Get some rest, you're going to need it."

I was headed for the door when Axle stopped me. I looked at him and he jerked his head towards his office. With a sigh, I followed him.

"I know Doc cleared you for duty. I just want to know if your head is in the game. If you need any additional time off let me know. I don't want the operation to fail or someone to get hurt." Axle said with concern.

"Do I look like a fucking pussy to you. The only reason I wasn't ready sooner was due to physical limitations. My head is screwed on just fine, fuck you very much." I growled at him. "I'm ready."

"Ok, I had to ask. You're right. I know you've got this." Axle said shaking his head. "I just know you will be worried about Lillian."

"I know Gears and Undertaker will protect them, so no I won't be worried about that." I told him, looking him in the eye. "I'll be here and ready for go time. Goodnight."

I headed back home to my girl. When I got there, I let myself in and found her asleep on the couch. She must have been trying to wait up for me. I locked the door, hung up my coat and then picked her up in my arms. She curled into me and tucked her head in my neck. I carried her to the bedroom and gently pulled off her leggings before tucking her under the covers. I stripped down and went to take a hot shower before crawling in bed beside her. I would do everything I could to make it home safely to her. I will never forget the shell of a person she was after her husband died. I don't want to be the cause of that kind of grief for her ever. When I came back to the bedroom, she was awake and watching me.

"I'm sorry baby, did I wake you up?" I asked her as she looked at me and licked her lips. "See something you like?"

"Yes, and it's my turn to play. Come here." She said to me raising up on her knees. I walked to the edge of the bed, and she put her arms around my neck and kissed me. Nipping and biting my lip before dipping her tongue inside my mouth to duel with my own, then she kissed down my neck slowly working her way down my chest and abs. She took time to lick along my tats, nipping and sucking as she went. By the time she got to my cock I was hard as a rock. I started to push her down, but she shook her head. "Nope, still my turn." I watched as she wrapped her little hand around the base of my cock and licked the crown before sucking it into her mouth. I placed my hands on her head gently. She moaned around my cock as she licked the underside and around flicking her tongue at the spot under the crown that was so sensitive. She kissed her way down pumping me with her hand as she took one of my balls into her mouth and rolled it around before giving the same attention to the other one. I was about to blow but she was enjoying herself and I didn't want to stop her. She looked up at me and winked at she took me back into her mouth and started working me down her throat with enthusiasm.

"Baby, if you don't want to swallow you need to move. I'm about to come down that lovely throat." I told her hoarsely. She just grabbed my ass and held me to her as I came. She didn't waste a drop. After licking me clean she sat back on her legs and smiled at me. "Damn."

"I wanted to give you pleasure the way you give me pleasure." She said as she laid back on the bed. I looked at her and noticed she was wet, her lips glistening with her arousal. She slid her hand down to her mound and then dipped it inside of her body, giving a couple of pumps and pulling her fingers out. I grabbed her hand and sucked her juices off of her fingers then slid down between her thighs to get my taste from the source.

"Looks like my girl likes sucking my cock." I said with a smirk as I licked around her pussy and up around her clit but not quite hitting it yet. She was moaning and writhing on the bed. "I want you to pinch your nipples for me while I eat you." She took direction really well as she ran her fingers around her breasts and then tweaked her nipples for me. I rewarded her by flicking her clit with my tongue and dipping two fingers into her soaking wet channel. She was so tight she squeezed my fingers. I reached inside and found her g-spot and tapped it while sucking her clit into my mouth making her come all over me.

"Oh my God, that was amazing." she said as she stared down at me with her eyes glistening and sweat on her brow. I raised up and flipped her over then slammed her back onto my cock. She screamed and started convulsing around me. Damn, I didn't want to come yet. I started trying to think of anything to stop me from blowing my load early. Deep breaths and then I grabbed her hips and started pumping in and out of her. I wet my thumb and started to work it in her taint. She started to pull back, but I smacked her ass, and she froze. I worked my thumb in and felt her squeeze me tighter. My girl likes me playing with her ass.

"Baby, have you ever been taken back here?" I asked her curiously. She shook her head no. "I'm going to own every bit of you eventually and I can't wait to take you here." I leaned over and kissed the back of her neck and then went back to working myself in and out of her. I was getting close, so I reached around and rubbed circles on her clit until she was coming and then I let myself go. Once we were able to breathe again, I gently pulled out of her and grabbed a couple of tissues to clean us up. Then I carried her to the bathroom and ran her a bubble bath. I turned off the water and then sat down in the tub with her on my lap. She leaned back against me, closing her eyes.

"Don't fall asleep baby. I'm going to wash you, but I also need to talk to you." I told her gently working the soapy cloth over her body. "You know we have a job out of town the day after tomorrow. The guy on the news was one of the ones who worked me over. I know his buddy is always with him. They retaliated against the Irish by killing a civilian. There is a manhunt for them, but we don't know if they are aware that I made it out of the clubhouse before the fire. We need you, Sophie, Annie, Bethann and the kids to stay at the clubhouse while we are gone. Undertaker and Gears are staying behind to protect all of you. Undertaker is retired from field work, but he stays in shape and can outshoot any of us. Gears is our IT guy we need him safe too. I would feel better if you stayed there. You can sleep in my room. Nobody has been using it since I've been staying here with you."

My girl was really quiet. I could feel her heart racing and I knew she was trying to process what I said. Finally, she looked back at me and nodded. Turning around in my arms she straddled me and sank down onto my cock. She slowly rode me until we both finished. I helped her out of the tub, and we dried off climbing into bed. I pulled her on top of me and wrapped my arms around her. She slept with her head on my pec. I lay there in the dark thinking while gently running my fingers up and down her back. Finally, I started to drift off to sleep.

9

Lillian

We got up the next morning and I was going to head over to Bethann and Hawks' place to watch the boys when Fury came in and told me we were working from the clubhouse this week. He said they set up laptops for us in the small conference room. I packed a bag for the week since we never knew how long they would be gone. We would sleep in his room at the clubhouse tonight and they would leave super early in the morning for their mission. I zipped up my bag and Fury grabbed it, putting it over his shoulder. He took my hand and we headed to his truck. I said I could walk but he refused saying it's too cold. He helped me into his truck and buckled me in before going around to get to the driver's side. We drove the short distance to the clubhouse and parked behind in one of the spots. Taking my bag and my hand he walked me inside. I saw Annie in the living room with Mattie and Bethann was there with her boys, so I walked over to say 'hi'. Cameron and Joshua waved at me from where they were playing with Mattie. I sat down with the girls to chat.

Fury went and dropped my bag off in his old room then went to the kitchen to talk to the guys. I watched him interacting with his brothers and smiled. I hated that he was going on this mission, but I understood that it is who he is. I would never try to change him.

"Well, by the look on your face, I am assuming things are going good between the two of you." Bethann said as she looked at me and then back at Fury who had turned to look at me. He smiled at me then winked and went back to his conversation. I blushed and turned back to watch the boys play.

"Yes, things are going really good with us. I wasn't looking for a relationship, but we seem to really understand each other. We get along well, like a lot of the same things." I said glancing back over at him. "He looks all gruff and mean but he is a gentleman. He never rushed me and was infinitely patient with me."

"He has been in love with you for a long time now." Annie said quietly. I started to protest but she shook her head. "All of us have seen it. It's in the way he doesn't see other women at all anymore. He watches you all the time, tries to make things easier for you. He warns off other guys he catches giving you the eye."

"I didn't realize. I just figured nobody wanted the sad widow." I said as our eyes met across the room. I gave him a little smile and then looked back at Annie.

"The tension between the two of you is so thick you could cut it with one his knives. The man is gone over you." She giggled and suddenly I was plucked off the couch. I squealed and Fury put me over his shoulder and carried me to his room.

He walked into the room and closed the door, locking it behind him. He put me down on the bed and started to strip off his clothes. My mouth got dry as I watched him. He never took his eyes off of me while he was stripping down.

"You will have to keep it down some with the kids in the other room, but I need you now." He said as he started to peel my clothes off of me. He started with my top, and I unclasped my bra, then he pulled off my boots and jeans. Licking his lips, he spread me open and started to eat me up. I was trying to be quiet and had to grab a pillow to bite down on to keep from moaning out loud. The man had a talented tongue, and I was coming in no time at all. Suddenly he rose up and pulled me down to him lining himself up and slowly pushing into me. He worked himself in and out of me at a slow pace, making me crazy. He smirked as I tried to work myself on him faster, but he had a firm grip on my hips and was in complete control.

"Please Brian, I need more." He grunted and started to pound into me faster until we both went over the edge. He reached over to his nightstand and pulled a couple of wipes out of a container to clean us up then tossed them into the trash. He lay beside me and pulled me into his arms.

"I like it when you call me by my real name. When it's just us, that's what I want you to call me baby." He told me as he held me tight to him. I reached up and kissed him and then rolled off the bed.

"I have to get dressed, I need to be helping with Cam and Josh so Bethann can work." I said as I looked around for my bra. He got up and helped me redress then got his clothes on. I was about to open the door when he put his hands on either side of my face and kissed me softly. "You're killing me baby."

"I have to get my fill before we go to tide me over until we get home." he said huskily. "We will pick this up again tonight." He smacked my ass and then opened the door. Blushing I went back to the area where the kids were playing. Annie was standing in the kitchen watching them and fixing breakfast. She smiled and winked when I came out. I walked over to the kitchen; we could see them play from there. The common room was a huge open area.

"Looks like you had some fun this morning. I figured I'd make a stack of pancakes and eggs for everyone. They will be in the planning stages today so they will get hungry." Annie said as she plated the next round of pancakes.

"I can help. I'm used to cooking for this bunch." I offered. She shook her head.

"You can do lunch, I have breakfast. Have some coffee and keep me company. The boys are fine over there, we can see them from here." She said, passing me a cup of coffee and the creamer. I poured myself a cup and sat back scanning the room. The guys had gone into their 'war room' to plan. Bethann and Sophie were in the little conference room working. We loaded the food into a couple of large warming dishes and grabbed a stack of plates and utensils walking towards the room they were in. We knocked and Hawk opened the door. When he saw the food, he smiled at us and took the heavy servers then Rider came and took the other. They came back to the door and gathered the plates and things. We had a carafe of coffee and they had disposable cups in the room.

"Thanks baby." Fury said as he gave me a quick kiss before they closed the door and went back to work. We went and fixed the kids a plate and got them situated at the table before sitting with them. Bethann and Sophie came in to eat with us. Undertaker was at the garage today working.

"Thanks for making breakfast. It's been a crazy morning. I have several accounts I'm working on and will be on a couple of calls soon, so this is perfect timing." Sophie said as she inhaled her food. "Bethann has been a godsend at work. She does ten times what Brittni used to do."

"Oh stop. If that's true, then they should have fired her a long time ago. I keep telling you I can do more" Bethann said shaking her head. "I love my job and I am so blessed to have friends like you."

"We are a big family. We look out for each other." Annie said smiling. She and Undertaker were such a sweet couple. She was his second chance love and he adored her. Despite the age gap between them, they were meant for each other. I had never seen him so happy.

"We are all so glad you are here Annie. Undertaker has been a new man since he found you and he adores Mattie." I said smiling at her. She smiled and looked down patting her stomach. I watched her for a minute and then had to ask. "Are you pregnant?"

"Yes, I'm due in July. We wanted to wait until I was through the first trimester before we said anything but now that we are we will start telling people." Annie smiled. I wondered what kind of daddy Brian would make. He was very attentive with me and seemed to do well around the kids. I didn't think I would ever be lucky enough to find someone else after Wolf died but now that I have, I think about all the possibilities.

"That's great, we will have to throw you a baby shower when it gets closer." Bethann said, getting up to rinse her plate and put it in the dishwasher. "I'm going for a refill and then back to work."

"I need to do the same." Sophie said quietly. I wondered why she was so sad. I'd make a point to ask her later when she wasn't working.

"Go ahead, I've got the dishes." I said as I cleared the rest of our plates and took them to the kitchen. We got the boys cleaned up and put them in the corner area watching Winnie the Pooh. I curled up with a book and Annie had some crocheting she was working on.

10

Fury

We sat around the table looking at the big screen on the wall. Gears had found street cameras to gather photos of the house where the kids were being held to await buyers. There were four girls ages four to nine, people were really fucking sick. We were determined to get in and get them out. The parents of three of the girls had been working with the police to try to find their kids. The mother of the four-year-old had been killed when they grabbed her. Her mother was poor and worked two jobs trying to support her daughter. She had just been picking her up from the sitter when the traffickers showed up to snatch the kids. Apparently, the woman that was keeping them had been working for the men finding young girls for them. She would be set up in an apartment complex where there were known to be several children needing sitters. She would advertise her services on the bulletin board. After several weeks she would notify the cartel of the ages of the children she was watching and send pictures. The young mother just happened to have the most erratic schedule and had shown up to pick up her daughter an hour early. She was shot in the head.

"Ok, Rider and Fang will go in the back door. There are two guards at each entrance and three inside. Blade and I will take them out from a distance. Hawk and Fury will go through the front after we take out the guards. We will be watching from both sides to be sure to get anyone that comes out if it's not one of you or the kids. Gator and Doc will be coming with a van as soon as we give the signal that it's clear. Doc can do preliminary checks of the children and then we will drop them off at the hospital after notifying the parents." Said Axle as he tapped on the table. "I want to be out the door by three am. We have a flight chartered leaving at five from Denver and I have arranged to have an SUV and a van made available as soon as we land. Get some rest."

"What about the little girl that was orphaned. She will be traumatized. I hate to see her put in the system." Fury said frowning.

"We will cross that bridge after we have them all safe." Axle ended the conversation by getting up and leaving the room.

"I guess that ends the meeting. I'm going to see my girl." Fury said as he walked out. I stepped into the common area and saw the boys were asleep in a couple of pack-n-plays that were set up close to the big fireplace. Annie and Lillian were watching a movie. I walked over and picked Lillian up and sat back down with her on my lap. She didn't utter a single complaint, she just laid her head on my chest and continued to watch the movie. I was content to sit and hold her. Annie looked over and smiled at us.

"I'm going to fix some sandwiches; we have a few boxes of chips in the pantry." Lillian said as she started to get up. "I can't fix them from your lap honey?"

"You don't need to worry about feeding everybody. The boys have eaten and everyone else here is an adult and capable of feeding themselves. I'm leaving in the morning, and I would like to spend the afternoon with my girl." I told her as I nuzzled her hair. She relaxed in my arms and sighed.

"I don't want to think about you leaving tomorrow. I hope you get all the kids back alive, but I'll worry until you get back home." she said quietly looking down at my hands around her. I wanted to reassure her, but I wouldn't lie or make promises that I wasn't sure I could keep. What we did was dangerous, and anything could happen. All I could do was promise to be extra careful and take every precaution to come home to her.

"Why don't the two of you go spend time together. I'll watch Cameron and Josh too. My man is staying behind so go ahead." Annie urged us. I smiled up at her and then hugged the woman.

"Thank you, I'd like that." Lillian said as she stood up and took my hand. I got up and followed her to our room. When she closed the door behind us, she locked it, then came over and crawled into my lap straddling me. "I know you can't make me any promises and I know better than most the dangers of your job. What you can promise me is that you won't take any unnecessary chances. You won't rush into a situation without evaluating it first. I thought the pain of losing Wolf would kill me, but it didn't. Then they took you and you came back to me hurt but you came back. I don't mind nursing you to health and bandaging your wounds as long as you come back." Lillian held my face in her hands and kissed me. She ate at my mouth like she was starving for me. I pulled back enough to strip off her shirt and bra then with an arm around her waist I flipped us, so I was on top and she was spread out on the bed. I kissed my way down her body slowly savoring every bit of her. She was so beautiful with her midnight black hair short around her face with little curls and those pale blue eyes that were misted with tears now. I kissed my way down her body pulling her pants down her legs and tossing them in the corner. She didn't have shoes on, she had kicked those off in the common area to watch the movie. Standing up I stripped my clothes off and threw them with hers in the corner. I don't know what I did to deserve her, but I was going to do my best to make sure she never regrets giving me a chance.

I wanted to worship her body slowly. I lay beside her and ran my hand over her neck tracing my way down between her breasts. I watched her face as I explored her body. She was panting and biting her lip. I smiled at her and continued, cupping her breasts one at a time flicking my thumb over her nipples. Still watching her I traced my way down her stomach so soft and along her pelvis to her mound. Her eyes were wide, and her pupils were dilated. She was writhing on the bed at this point. I traced along her labia down to her taint. She gasped and moved closer to my hand.

"Please Brian." She begged as she could no longer keep still, and her legs were shaking.

"What do you need baby?" I asked her as I ran my fingers through her soaked folds up to her clit. She moaned and tried to use her hand to guide mine. "Put your hands over your head and use your words."

"Please let me come." She begged looking at me with lust filled eyes and flushed skin. She was magnificent in her arousal, and I wanted to watch her come apart for me. I slid a finger inside her and pumped, her breathing quickened. Then I slipped a second finger in and used my thumb on her clit. After a few thrusts she came apart. I felt a rush of fluid coat my hand as I watched her orgasm roll through her. I pulled my fingers out and sucked her juices from them then I mounted her and pulled her legs around my waist. I lined myself up with her entrance then entwined my hands with hers and slid slowly inside. She was still contracting around my cock, and it took everything in me not to come too quickly. I started counting in my head getting control of myself then I started to fuck her hard. She squeezed my hands and looked me in the eye. I felt it then as I came hard and looked in her eyes. I was in love with this woman. I haven't looked at another woman in months. She is it for me. I gently pulled out and went to get us a damp cloth to clean up with. When I came back, she had not moved. I cleaned her up and tossed the cloth in the bathroom. Then laid down beside her to hold her. Pulling her onto my chest so I could hold her as close as possible.

"That was amazing, I can see why you are so popular with the ladies." Lillian said quietly. "If I see another woman touch you, I'll have to beat her ass."

I chuckled and pulled her up for a kiss. "What women? I don't see any other woman but you."

"Good, best you keep it that way Brian Nash." she giggled at me. I was thinking about another round when her stomach let out a growl.

"I think I need to feed my girl, she is going to need her energy tonight." I said as I smacked her ass and rolled her on her side. I got up and slipped on my jeans and a shirt tossing another one of my shirts to her. She pulled it over her head and snagged her jeans off the floor. I took her hand and led her into the kitchen so we could fix a late lunch. Annie had taken the boys to one of the spare rooms to play so nobody was in the common room right now. I know some of the guys were getting things together and a couple were probably getting some before we take off. Lillain was fixing us sandwiches when Axle's door opened and one of the strippers came out looking well used. I recognized her from some of the parties we have on occasion. I couldn't remember her name although I'm pretty sure I have tapped that before. She smiled when she saw me and sauntered over. Well shit.

"Fury, long time no fuck?" she said as she ran a finger down my arm. "Want to go to your room for a bit?" I grabbed her hand and removed it from my arm.

"Don't touch me again." I said in a hard voice. I knew Lillian was watching from the kitchen. "I'm involved with someone, and I don't like sloppy seconds anyway."

She tried again to get close to me, but Lillian stepped between us pushing her away from me. I wrapped my arms around my girl and glared at the piece of trash standing there.

"I think it's best you leave. Axle is clearly got what he wanted and is done with you. Fury doesn't want you. Best you get out of here." Lillian said with authority.

"Who the hell are you to tell me to leave." The woman said huffing. Just then we heard a door slam and Axle walked across the room.

"Jackie, I told you to leave." Axle snapped at her. "You served your purpose but now you need to go. You know the rules around here."

"Why does she get to stay?" Jackie whined pointing to Lillian. She was gearing up for a fight that would get her banned from the property permanently.

"She's my old lady, she can do what the fuck she wants." I said fiercely as I squeezed Lillian's hip so she wouldn't say anything yet. "You are not to touch me or talk to me ever again. I'd also advise you not to go near my girl."

"Fine, whatever I'm leaving. Call me when you get bored with Little Miss Muppet." She hissed as she walked off. Lillian looked up at me then turned to go back to the kitchen to finish fixing lunch.

"Damn, sorry about that man. I didn't know she was going to act like that." Axle apologized. "So, you make it official?" he nodded at Lillian.

"No but I need to fix that since I declared it before asking her." I said walking over to her and taking a seat at the counter.

11

*L*illian

I was stunned into silence by Fury's declaration. You don't claim a woman as your old lady unless you mean it. It's not a nickname or a casual thing. It's as good as saying she is your wife or intended. My head was reeling as I fixed our lunch. I would never embarrass him by calling him out in front of anyone, but we needed to have a conversation. Axle left, probably heading to his house to pack his bag for their mission. Fury took his regular seat at the kitchen counter. He just watched me waiting for me to finish and sit with him. Placing our plates beside each other I put a bottle of water out for each of us and then sat down. I took a bite of my chips and waited.

"You mad?" he asked as he looked over at me. "I should have talked to you before I did that."

"You should have, but no, I'm not mad." I looked at him and took his hand. "I never thought I'd be someone's old lady again. It took me by surprise, but not in a bad way."

"I was going to talk to you about it after we got back from this mission, but she just pissed me off and I wanted it clear who you are to me. I wanted you to know too." Fury said sheepishly. I looked at this fierce, strong man and my heart just melted. He could be so scary with other people and could snap someone into pieces with that chain of his, but I knew he would never hurt me. I was sure he would guard me with his life. He also was quick to claim me in front of the club whore who hit on him. He made it clear that I was the only one he wanted.

"I was surprised but proud that you claimed me in front of her and in front of your club president. That makes me feel so much better about all these feelings I have for you." I told him blushing. I took a bite of my sandwich because I was starving and because I wanted to go back to our room. He squeezed my knee as he ate his food. He grinned like a cheshire cat that had gotten his way.

"I want you to be my wife and old lady. I want a future with you and a family with you. If that's what you want." he said hesitantly. I knew he was concerned due to me having lost a baby before, but I did want kids still. I'd love to have a family with him however that looks.

"I'd love to have a family with you and yes, I want to be your wife and your old lady. I'd be proud to wear your cut." I told him before he lifted me off the stool spinning me around in a circle. I giggled at his reaction. He looked up at me and kissed me.

"My old lady. I really like the sound of that. I'll see about having your cut made and we can discuss plans to make this all official when I get back. Just know that I love you. I have for quite a while; I just didn't want to scare you away. I knew you needed time." Fury sat me back down in my seat. "Finish your lunch you will need your energy."

We finished eating and then went to our room. He was right, I definitely used a lot of energy before we fell asleep for the evening. I woke up the next morning to a note by the bed and Fury gone. I knew they left super early and I was worn out from our activities last night. I grabbed his pillow and pulled it to me taking a deep whiff of his cologne. My body was deliciously sore. I got up and took a shower getting ready for the day. I was going to help Annie with the boys and try to keep my mind off of what the men were off doing.

Making breakfast for the kids took my mind off of it for a bit. They were sitting at the table the two little ones in their booster seats playing with their cars while they waited. I made French toast this morning with bananas and whipped cream, I also had some bacon fixed to go along with it. Annie was feeling a bit nauseous this morning so I told her I would take care of them while she slept in some. They were being good, I put their sippy cups with milk in front of them and a plate cut up with their breakfast. I sat down with them to eat. Undertaker, Gears, Sophie and Bethann wandered in and fixed a plate. Gears, Sophie and Bethann thanked me for cooking and took theirs back in to work. Undertaker sat and ate with us. Playing with the boys and doing planes to feed them some. They all laughed.

"You doin' okay Lil?" Undertaker asked me. He was still president when I married Wolf, it was not long before his wife passed. I had been close to Lisa. She was a nice lady. He tried to check on me as much as he could, but we were both in a bad place.

"I'm okay. Just trying to stay busy this morning. You know?" I said glancing at the kids. I didn't want them to pick up on the fact that I was worried. Cameron and Josh had lost so much already, and they loved Hawk as a father. The little ones were too young to understand that anything was going on but Cameron was very perceptive for his age.

"Ms. Lily, can I go watch Paw Patrol?" Cameron asked as he finished his last bite of bacon. The little ones were almost done eating too.

"Wait just a couple of minutes for Mattie and Josh to finish then you three can watch Paw Patrol and play with your legos." I told them.

"Why don't you go wash your hands and use the bathroom while you wait for them."

"Yes, ma'am." He said politely as he climbed down from the table. I watched him head to the bathroom off the side of the kitchen. We had a step stool in there for when the kids were here.

"Congrats on the pregnancy. I hope you end up with a little girl." I said with a twinkle in my eye. Undertaker looked horrified, which made me laugh.

"Don't say that. What would I do with a little girl?" he said looking at the boys. I got up and wet a washcloth and wiped the boy's mouths and hands then put them down to go play. We took their dishes to the kitchen, and I washed them before finishing clean up.

"You were great with Lucy's little girl whenever they came to visit. She adores you Uncle Santa." I teased. He blushed and shook his head. "Sarah adores you."

"She is a sweet little girl, very well behaved." He said smiling thinking of Stone and Lucy's daughter. They lived in the next town over, so they didn't get by very often. They needed to have a cookout when it warmed up and they could invite Bear and his family as well as their other friends. "The guys will be fine. Fury is great in the field. He is crazy about you, so he is going to be even more careful, so he comes home to you."

"I know what happened to Wolf wasn't the norm and that they shot him up close. It doesn't make it any easier and I can't help but worry about Fury. I'll feel a little better when he calls to check in." I said as I dried my hands and sat down on the couch. Zeke 'Undertaker' sat in the armchair watching his son. Mattie was like a carbon copy of him. I was so happy that he had found someone to love who adores him and can give him the family he always wanted. Annie came out of one of the guest rooms about a half hour later and came to sit in his lap. I got up and got her some crackers and ginger ale. I remembered that it helped when she was sick with Mattie.

"Thanks Lil?" she murmured around the cracker. "My stomach has been so off; I'm still trying to see what I can eat that doesn't upset it."

"If you would like I could start keeping Mattie for you while you work. He and Josh play really well together." I suggested. They both smiled at me.

"That would be great, are you sure it wouldn't be too much?" Annie asked me with a hopeful expression on her face.

"It's fine. I enjoy having them." I told her. We chatted a bit and watched the boys playing. A little while later they started yawning so I put them all down for a nap. They decided to take a nap while the kids were out, so I curled up on the couch to read a book.

12

Fury

We had pulled up near the house that we believed the kids were being held in about two hours ago. We sent Blade and Axle to do some recon, so we knew for sure how to strike. I was hoping to do this as quietly as possible; we didn't want the children to be any more traumatized than they already were. They would be in position with their sniper rifles to take out the guys at the front door and back. It was dark out when we got the go ahead to move in.

Hawk and I were headed to the front while Rider and Fang went to the back. The guards they had were nothing more than hired muscle. They were taken down easily without having to kill them. We cuffed them and tied their legs up leaving them out of sight. Then we went inside. There were two men in the living room that pulled guns and we took them out quickly. We searched for the other guy and found him in the room with the kids. He was trying to touch one of the little girls who was crying and shaking. I looked at her and held my finger to my lips and told her to close her eyes. Rider got him with a silencer, and it knocked him away from her. Fang pulled him out into the room with the others we had to kill.

"Doc, we're ready for the van. We also need to radio for clean up." I said into the hand radio.

"Be there in five." Doc said before disconnecting. The four of us in the house each picked up one of the kids and carried them out. Holding their heads against our chest so they wouldn't see the carnage. When we came out my little brother was standing beside the SUV. We loaded the kids into the vehicle and when Doc pulled up a couple of the guys went and dragged the men in cuffs to the van. We secured them in the van and then headed for the hospital. We had alerted them that we were coming in and bringing children that needed to be checked out for injuries and rape. They would have a counselor on hand and the state police would meet us there for a debriefing before they took the men into custody.

I carried the little one in and went to put her down on one of the exam tables, but she wouldn't let go of me. Instead, I sat down in a chair with her on my lap and tried to talk to her.

"Your name is Emma, right?" I asked as I rubbed her little back. "My name is Fury, or you can call me Brian." She was trembling in my arms, and I wanted to go back and rip those guys to shreds again. She sat back and looked at me.

"Is the bad man dead?" she asked watching my face. "I want my mommy."

I felt a punch in my gut. She was the youngest one, her mother was killed when they took her. I don't know if she saw anything or not. I sat her sideways so I could see her face.

"Emma, do you remember what happened when the bad men took you?" I asked her gently. Her little face crumpled, and she started to sob. I held her to me and rocked her.

"They hurt my mommy. She fell down and was bleeding. I want to see my mommy." She said between sobs. Damn, I hated this. A lady doctor came into the room and looked over to see her in my lap. She looked at her with sympathy.

"Hi, are you Emma Grace? My name is Dr. Casey. I need to check you for boo boos." The doctor kneeled down in front of us. "Can you sit on the bed for me Emma?"

She shook her little head and clung tighter to me. I looked up at the sympathy on her face. I shook my head.

"Can you start her check up with her in my lap?" I asked her. "I carried her out and I think she feels safe with me."

"That's fine, you can stay with Mr. Nash. Can you open your mouth so I can check your temperature?" she asked her. Emma looked at the nice doctor and opened her mouth. Her temperature was normal, so she checked her ears and throat next. She had a few scrapes and bruises that she cleaned and bandaged. I knew she wanted to be sure she had not been violated. I wasn't sure because when we walked in the man was trying to touch her.

"Emma, can you tell me where the bad man touched you?" I asked her gently. She shook her head. "You don't have to say it, just point for me." She bit her lip and pointed to her chest. "Anywhere else?" she shook her head no.

"You're doing really good Emma. Would you like a clean gown to wear?" she asked, and the little girl just shook her head and clung to me. "Ok, I'm going to go check on your friends and I'll be back in a minute."

Axle tapped at the door, and I looked up at him. He saw the child clinging to me and smiled. It was a sad smile, we had to tell her about her mother, but she was already so traumatized we didn't want to make it worse.

"We are taking off in a couple of hours." Axle said watching me. I shook my head.

"I may be here a little longer. She needs me right now." I continued to rub her little back until I felt her go limp in my arms. I realized she was finally asleep. I stood up slowly and eased her under the blanket on the bed. I stepped away to talk to Axle.

"I need to call Lillian. I want to let her know that we are alright, and I am thinking about seeing if we can adopt her. She doesn't have any family; she saw her mother killed and she has attached herself to me. I know that Lillian wants kids, and she has a good heart. This little girl needs a stable home and family." I told him as I watched her sleep. Her red hair was matted, and she had bright green eyes and the most adorable freckles across her little nose. I think she already had me wrapped around her little finger.

"I'll talk to the social worker and state police. We have a little pull with them. I think I can make that happen. You need to call Lillian first and make sure she is on board." Axle said as he glanced at the little girl in the bed cuddled to my jacket.

"Do me a favor. I don't want to leave and have her wake up with me not here. Will you go down to the gift shop and get her a stuffie?" I asked him, handing him some cash.

"Ok, shoot me a text as soon as you confirm with Lily." Axle said as he slapped me on the shoulder. "Look at you. Getting married and already starting a family."

"Get the fuck out of here." I said flipping him off. I went and sat down by the bed and called my girl.

She answered on the first ring. She sounded all sleepy and I wished I was there with her.

"Brian, you're okay. I miss you so much. When are you coming home?" she said in a rush. I smiled at her question.

"Yes baby, it went according to plan. There is one little hiccup though. How would you feel about having a four-year-old daughter?" I asked her, holding my breath.

"What are you talking about?" she asked sounding confused. "Sure, I want kids, are you wanting to adopt?"

"One of the girls is an orphan, her mother was killed during the initial kidnapping. She has no other family, and she has kind of attached herself to me. I don't think I can leave her for the system." I said waiting for her response.

"Well of course you can't. Bring that baby home." She said adamantly. I smiled that's my girl. "I'll order some stuff for her now. I'll have it overnighted to the clubhouse. Let me know when you will be home. I love you."

"I love you too Lil, I'll call you in the morning with the details. Goodnight baby." I said as I hung up. I started to shoot a text to Axle when he walked in with a stuffed elephant. It was rainbow colored, soft and squishy. I took the tag off and put it next to her in the bed.

"I heard. I already made the arrangements. I knew she would say yes." He said smirking. We will wait and fly home tomorrow afternoon when they release her. They pulled some strings and got you custody. We just have to finalize everything at home once you and Lillian get married."

I stared at the little girl who would be my daughter. I wanted to spoil her rotten. I knew we would have to get her counseling and be incredibly patient with her. I just hoped she would adjust well to her new life.

"Don't worry, we will get her all the help she needs. I sent Hawk to pick up a couple of things for her to have to wear home. Get some rest." Axle said and he left closing the door behind him.

"My mommy went to heaven, didn't she?" a little voice asked softly. I looked over at Emma. She was looking at me with sad little eyes and a quivering lip. "I saw the bad man shoot her. She didn't get up and there was a lot of blood. Then they took me away."

I walked over to the bed, picked her up and sat down with her on my lap. I would not lie to her.

"Yes, little bit, she went to heaven." I told her. "Don't worry you are coming home with me. My girl and I will give you a good home. Would that be okay with you?"

Emma looked up at me in surprise. Suddenly her little arms were around my neck, and she was sobbing her little heart out. I rubbed her back and rocked her. The nurse came in and wanted to check her again. They brought her some food and some chocolate milk.

"I found a lady's small scrub top. I thought maybe she could sleep in that until she had some clothes to change into." The nurse was super nice. She brought a washcloth and basin over to help clean her up. "Would you like me to wash your hair sweet pea? We can do it in the sink, you can just lean your head over it. I'll wash it and brush it out then braid it for you."

"Will you stay with me?" she asked me, looking back and forth between us. I nodded and she agreed. We went into the bathroom, and she stood in a chair leaning over the sink. I had a towel for her to hold over her eyes. I wet her hair down and reached for the shampoo from the nurse. After putting a little in my hands, I massaged it into her hair being careful not to get it in her eyes. After working it through well, I rinsed it out and repeated the process. Wrapping a towel around her head I carried her into the room and helped her sit on the bed.

"Why don't you try to eat while she brushes out your hair?" I suggested. Emma looked up at me and again at the nurse. "Do you want to use this washcloth to wipe your face off?" She took the washcloth and wiped her face, then her arms and legs. I took it and put it in the basin in the bathroom. She looked at the scrub top and at me. "I'll turn around and you can change into the top. You will have some clean clothes to wear home tomorrow."

"Ok." She said as I turned to face the wall. A few minutes later she tugged on my shirt. I turned around and she was eating her grilled cheese sandwich. After she finished eating, she laid down and I covered her up handing her the elephant. "Where did he come from?"

"I had my friend get him for you. You want to name him?" I asked her. She nodded. Looking at her elephant she thought for a few minutes and said "Sprinkles".

"That's a good name. How about you and Sprinkles get some sleep, and I will be here all night." I told her. She curled up on her side holding the stuffie and watched me until her eyes got heavy and she fell asleep.

"I'll bring you a blanket and a pillow for that recliner. It gets cool in these rooms at night." The nurse said eyeing me up and down. I picked up my phone and sent a message to my girl, letting her know we would be home tomorrow evening.

13

*L*illian

When I spoke to Fury earlier, I almost passed out. We were going to be parents. Hell, we just got engaged. I mean I knew that I loved him and wanted to be with him, and we have been living together for weeks but just WOW. As soon as I hung up, I went online and ordered furniture for her room. I had a three-bedroom house and the room closest to ours was empty. It was painted pale yellow. We could change it later if she wanted but for now it would do. I ordered a twin-size day bed, a matching nightstand and dresser. I looked online and saw a cute multicolored throw rug, with a matching lamp and curtains. I ordered those to be delivered overnight. I also got bedding to match. I wanted her to have some toys, so I picked out a barbie doll house along with furniture and some barbies. We could pick up a few things once she gets here. Then I picked out a few outfits. I didn't want to get too much until I was sure of her sizes. It was supposed to be delivered by noon tomorrow. I would have a couple of the prospects go set it up at our house.

"Looks like somebody is doing some shopping. Are those kids clothes and toys?" Annie asked me surprised. I blushed and nodded.

"One of the girls they rescued is now an orphan, her mother was killed during the kidnapping. She has no other family so Fury arranged for us to adopt her." I told her as I sat back and just stared at the stuff I had just bought. "She kind of attached herself to him after he carried her out. Apparently, my man is smitten with this little girl. I hope she likes me. I want to be a good mother to her."

"I'm sure you will be. You're great with our kids. She will have some time before she has to start school so she can get used to you." Bethann said as she hugged me. "You're gonna be a Mama. That's awesome."

"It is, isn't it. I can't quite wrap my head around it." I said wrapping my arms around myself. "I think I'm going to take a shower and go to bed; tomorrow is going to be a busy day."

"It is, goodnight, Lillian. Let us know if we can help." Annie said. "With anything."

"I will, thanks." I told them as I went to our room and closed the door. Instead of a shower I decided to take a bath. The hot water would help me relax. I pulled one of Fury's t-shirts and a pair of his boxers out to sleep in then started the bath. When it was ready, I settled down and leaned against the back. I closed my eyes and thought about the last two months. They were great, we got along well and made a great team. I understand him the way he understands me. The chemistry between us is off the charts. I know we can do this. I would look for a counselor first thing. She would need help adjusting to her new reality and the loss of her mother. I felt sleepy so I got out of the tub, dried off and got ready for bed. I pulled his pillow close and got comfortable. I was out like a light.

The next morning, I was up with the chickens. I was so wound up for the day that I couldn't relax. I got up and dressed in warm clothes then went to the kitchen to fix a pot of coffee. The boys would be up in a bit, so I made a huge batch of cinnamon rolls and laid some fruit out. Sitting down at the counter with a roll and some coffee I scrolled through my phone and reread the last message that Fury sent me. He had snapped a picture of Emma Grace for me. She was adorable. I felt my heart melt at the sight of the little girl curled up on the bed. Her little fist under her chin. I saw the stuffie and figured it was a gift from my guy. He could be such a bad ass but when it came to children, he was a pushover. Seeing the rainbow elephant made me feel good about my decorating choices for her room. The things I ordered were from the next town over at a Department Store. I paid for the expedited delivery for this morning. I wanted to have her room together before she arrived. Undertaker came out of one of the bedrooms first. He was in his late forties and a handsome devil. I had known him a long time. He smiled when he saw me sitting at the counter. He came over to give me a hug and get a cup of coffee.

"You're an angel for making coffee and I smell cinnamon buns." He sniffed the air and looked at the stove. Lifting the towel, he snagged one and put it on a plate. Sitting down across from me with the sticky bun and coffee he took a bite and groaned. "You always could bake like nobody else. I hear we will have another little one running around here. How are you feeling about that?"

"I'm excited and terrified all at the same time. I was starting to wonder if I would ever have kids after…" I trailed off looking out towards the window. "Well anyway, I hope that I will be a good mom to her. I think she has already wrapped Fury around her finger."

"I have no doubt. He is crazy about Mattie and has grown attached to Hawk and Bethann's boys as well. I don't think he ever imagined he would be a father." Undertaker finished his bun and took a drink of his coffee. He got up and washed his dish, putting it in the sink. I watched him fix a glass of ginger ale and grab a sleeve of crackers. "I'm going to take these to Annie before she tries to get up. It helps to settle her stomach if she eats some and has her ginger ale before she gets out of bed. If you need anything let me know."

"Thank you, we will." I replied as I watched head back to his girl and their little one. He was such a good dad. I was happy for them that they were expecting again. Mattie was such a sweet little boy. A few minutes later Cam and Josh padded out with Bethann behind them. They ran over to me and hugged me.

"Good morning, would you little monkeys like a cinnamon bun?" I asked them. They both nodded their heads and went to the table. Bethann laughed and fixed them some milk while I got their buns on a small plate to put in front of them. I had also cut up some strawberries and bananas to go with it. "Be sure to eat your fruit."

"So what time is the stuff supposed to be here? A couple of the prospects have already offered to put the furniture together for you. We can wash the sheets and clothes before she arrives." Bethann said as we watched the boys devour their breakfast.

"It should be here by ten, I figured I would go over to the house with them long enough to show them where to put everything." I kept looking at my watch. I knew I had a couple of hours before it arrived, but I was anxious for something to do.

"Let's get the boys and watch a movie with them. By the time the movie is over they will be ready for nap and the furniture should be delivered. Gears will be here with Sophie, Bethann, the boys and myself. Zeke can go with you to the house." Annie said as she got the kids settled on the floor in front of the television and put in one of their favorite movies. We sat back to watch with them. My phone beeped and I looked down to see a message from Fury.

Fury: *Hey baby, we are getting ready to board the plane. We will be there early afternoon. Can't wait to see you.*

Lillian: *I'll have the room ready when you get here. I can't wait to meet her. Can't wait to see you too. Be safe.*

I put my phone back on the end table and curled up to watch the movie. Josh climbed onto the couch and laid his head in my lap. I played with his hair while he watched the movie. I couldn't believe I was going to have a daughter today. Fury had told me that we would have to finalize the adoption, but the FBI had pulled some strings to help. She was a little older than Cameron and it would be fun to see her interact with the younger kids. We would need to be patient with her and show her a lot of affection. I noticed the movie had been cut off and all three boys had fallen asleep. Annie went to grab blankets to throw over them. We put them in the play pens to sleep. I got a notification on my phone that the delivery truck was in front of my house.

I got my purse and Undertaker walked over with me. A couple of the prospects were there already talking to the driver and his helper. The guys were determined that no strangers were to come inside my home, so they had the guys pull the furniture out of the truck and our guys took it in and put it together. I showed them where I wanted everything, and it took them about fifteen minutes to assemble the bed. The rest were already together. We laid the rug down beside the bed. I put the lamp on the nightstand and went to get a light bulb to put in it. There were some toys and clothes that would be here a little later. They were sent overnight express. I figured eventually we would take her to pick out some things, but she needed time to get comfortable first. I had the clothes and toys delivered to the clubhouse, so we didn't have to wait here. About the time we headed back I saw the UPS driver pull up with the rest of the packages. I ran to see them, but Undertaker grabbed me around the waist and pulled me back. I looked up and he shook his head.

"You don't know if they are safe. Wait and let us get the boxes and bring them inside. Please." He said with an eyebrow raised. I blushed and nodded. I knew better, I was just excited.

"I'm sorry." I said sheepishly looking up at him. "I'm just excited to get things ready for her."

"I know you are, and we will. Go have a seat at the table and we will bring them in." he told me and gave me a nudge toward the door. I walked inside and the ladies came out to help. The guys brought the boxes in after they opened them to be sure there wasn't anything in the boxes that should not be there, then they put them on the table for us to go through. We pulled out the sheets and some of her clothes separating them to start a small load. The dollhouse needed to be put together, but I was pretty sure Fury would want to do that for her. There were some baby doll items like a bed and stroller as well as a little doll.

"Do you have a toy box?" Bethann asked me. I looked up in surprise, I didn't think about that. "It's no big deal, I have an extra wicker laundry basket that you can use. I'll grab it and we can put some of the stuff in it to carry to the house.

"There is just so much to know. It's been a long time since I gave any thought to being a mom and having a child around my house. It helps that I have been keeping yours." I told her as she hugged me.

"We've got you. Don't worry, if you need anything give us a call. If we don't have it, we can get it." Annie said with a big smile. She rubbed her belly. We fixed the kids some lunch and got them up from their naps. Josh was doing really good with his potty training since he has been able to copy Cameron. It has made it easier. We fed the boys, and I had the toys by the door. Fury would let me know when he was almost home and one of the guys would walk me and help carry all the stuff to my house to be there to greet them. I went to switch out the clothes and start one more load. I just washed the bedding and some pajamas for her for tonight along with panties and socks. I would wash the rest at home. We gathered the stuff together and carried it over. I went in and made the bed and laid out the pajamas on the bottom of the bed for her. Then I went to start another load of laundry while I waited for them to arrive. Undertaker was watching television.

14

Fury

One of the nurses had a granddaughter that was Emma's age and the same size, so she brought in a couple pairs of jeans, some cute sweatshirts, T-shirts, socks and undies. We also managed to get her a pair of boots. The nurse helped her get ready, and we brushed out her hair and put it in pigtails. I sent Hawk to Walmart for a coat that she could wear. We were sitting in the chair with her on my lap watching cartoons on the tv while we waited for her discharge papers. I had texted Lillian a couple of times to keep her updated and I showed Emma a few pictures I had taken of Lillian over the last month since I started getting around better. She touched the picture and looked at me. I knew she missed her mother. I couldn't do anything about that.

Emma was very quiet. I had been around a lot of traumatized kids over the years, so I was used to them being quiet and introverted after being kidnapped and abused in different ways. Thankfully other than just a little inappropriate touching nothing more serious had happened before we got to her. It was still inexcusable and horrific, but it could have been so much worse. She was going to have nightmares and need a lot of therapy, having also witnessed her mother's murder.

"Do you think she will like me?" Emma asked me in her sweet little voice. "Are you sure she will want me?" I could hear the insecurity in her voice. She was afraid that she would be abandoned again.

"Yes poppet, Lily will adore you. She loves kids." I told her as I rubbed her little back to comfort her. She leaned against me and sighed. "We want you to stay with us and be our little girl. There is no pressure. We just want you to know you have a home with us forever."

"Ok, thank you Mr. Fury." she said softly. She clutched the stuffie under her chin and closed her eyes. I knew she was still exhausted.

"Why don't you call me Papa or any other kind of father like name you want." I suggested to her.

"Ok, Papi." She said in a sleepy voice. The doctor came in with the paperwork, he told me that usually the nurse did the discharge, but he wanted to check on her one more time. Since she was sleeping, he just left me with some vitamins, antibiotics and some liquid Tylenol to take with us. A few minutes later Hawk showed up with her coat. He picked a bright pink one with white fur around the hat and sleeves. He also had a soft, fluffy pink blanket in his arms.

"My boys like their personal blankets and I figured she could sleep on the plane. We are meeting the others at the airfield." Hawk said as he held the coat up for me to slip her arms in. She didn't stir. We got her coat on and zipped up. I stood with her in my arms, and we wrapped the blanket around her. Hawk grabbed the bag with her things, and we headed out.

After I got her buckled up in her booster seat, I slid in the back beside her in case she woke up scared. I wanted her to know I was close. We had about a thirty-minute drive to the air strip, so we chatted quietly.

"I bet Lillian is beside herself waiting for you to get home. I'm sure she is going to spoil little Emma rotten. The boys already have her wrapped around their fingers." Hawk winked at me when he said it. "You have been so good with her. I'm glad you two are going to take her and give her a home."

"I had already planned to eventually ask Lillian to marry me, but this will speed things up a bit." I told him as I glanced at a picture of my girl on my phone. She was smiling with her dark hair curling around her face, her eyes sparkling, and her cheeks flushed from the cold. She was stunning. I was a lucky man. I just had to make sure she knows how lucky I feel.

We pulled up and got out. I got Emma out of the booster seat and Hawk grabbed the seat and the bag with her things. I carried her onto the airplane and then got her settled in a seat beside me. I made sure to roll up a blanket and pillow to prop her head on. She was so exhausted from everything she had been through.

The doctor told me she may sleep a lot for a few days up to a week. He said naps are a good idea and of course counseling. The other guys were quiet around her so as not to wake her up. I sent a text to Lily to let her know we were taking off and then I laid back and closed my eyes to nap. We touched down and we had two SUV's waiting for us at the airport. Hawk, Rider and I rode in one with Emma and Axle, Blade, Fang and Doc rode in the other. I texted Lillian that we were almost there.

Emma woke up as we arrived at the compound, she looked around and saw the fence and guard shack as well as the guys at the gate. She looked at me and frowned.

"They are here to keep you safe. They don't let anybody on our property that we don't know or trust." I assured her as she looked back out the window. She seemed to relax after I told her that. I'm sure it would be a while before she felt safe. I just hoped that she would feel safe with us.

"Ok Papi." She looked up and saw Lillian at the door to her house as we pulled up. Hawk parked and I got out reaching for Emma. I kept her on my hip as I walked over to Lily. Emma had a death grip on my shirt and her face tucked into my neck.

"Hey baby, I missed you." I said as I wrapped my other arm around her and gave her quick kiss on the lips. Then she stepped back and bit her lip looking at the little girl in my arms. "Hey Poppet, can you say hello to Lily?"

Lillian stood there patiently giving her time to decide for herself. Emma slowly raised her head and clutching her stuffie to her chest she gave Lily a little smile. "Hello."

"Hello Emma, I'm Lily. I'm so glad to meet you. What is your friends name?" she asked Emma pointing to the stuffie in her arms.

"This is Sprinkles, she's my best friend." She said quietly. "My Papi got it for me in the hospital." Lillian looked at me when she heard the nickname and I saw tears in her eyes. She smiled trying to blink them back.

"It's really cold out here, how about we get you and Sprinkles inside where it's warm?" Lily asked her, waiting for her response. Emma just nodded. Hawk handed Lily the bag and left us to bond. "I don't know what you like to eat so I thought I could make us some grilled cheeses and chicken noodle soup for dinner."

"I like noodle soup and grilled cheese. My mommy used to make it a lot." Her little lip quivered, and she tucked her head back into Fury's neck and sniffled. He rubbed her little back and sat down on the couch with her in his lap. My girl looked so sad, she went to the kitchen and fixed our dinner. We figured she would likely go to bed early. I turned on the Disney channel and found a movie. She seemed to like Moana, so I left it on that.

"Poppet, do you need to use the bathroom?" I asked her. Her eyes got wide, and she nodded. I pointed to the bathroom. "It is that door just past the kitchen. Make sure you wash your hands when you finish." I got up and walked to the kitchen and wrapped my arms around Lily. "Baby, are you okay?" I whispered in her ear.

"Yes, my heart just breaks for her. We can talk more later for now let's just help her feel comfortable here." She said as she pulled out a bowl and plate with Moana on it and a matching sippy cup. I noticed there were several different princess sets in the cabinet. I kissed her cheek, and we heard the toilet flush and the water run, then Emma came back into the living room. She looked at us and smiled. She walked over to the table and glanced shyly at Lillian then started to climb on the chair at the table. I picked her up and settled her in the booster seat. When she saw the dishes, she smiled so big.

"I love Moana. She is my favorite." Emma was still holding her stuffie and I suggested we put it on the chair beside her while she eats so that nothing gets on her. "Ok Sprinkles, you sit in this chair and be good."

We all sat down and ate a late lunch of grilled cheese sandwiches and chicken noodle soup. It was a nice meal on a cool day. Emma must have been hungry because she cleaned her plate and bowl. She got up and took her plate and bowl to the sink and looked around.

"What are you looking for Emma?" Lillian asked her gently. She was trying to tread carefully with the child and not crowd her.

"I had a stool at home so I could reach the sink. I need to wash my dishes." She said looking around still. "I got in trouble if I didn't clean up my own dishes at Ms. Beards house."

I noticed she was trembling and suddenly looked scared. I got up and picked her up to sit her in my lap.

"You don't have to do dishes here. When you are older you will have some chores like any other kid but for now taking your dishes to the sink is good enough." I gave her a hug. "Why don't you and Sprinkles go watch a movie and I'll clean up the dishes."

She looked at me with wide eyes then hugged me and hopped down. Lily was watching us and smiling. I looked at her a little embarrassed and shrugged my shoulders.

"Emma, can I watch the movie with you?" Lily asked her as she walked to the couch. Emma nodded and patted the seat beside her. I watched my girls sitting on the sofa watching a Disney movie and my heart had never felt so full. I would love to give her a few more kids.

I quickly cleaned up the kitchen. I was going to use the dishwasher but since she liked this dish set so much, I wanted it to be clean for her next meal so I handwashed it. When I was done, I went to sit with them and watch the movie.

15

Lillian

We were all relaxed on the sofa watching Moana when I noticed she had laid her head down in Fury's lap and was rubbing her eyes. The movie was almost over so I went to run her a bubble bath. After getting the bath ready, putting a few toys in it and gathering her nightclothes I went to the living room to get her.

"Emma, let's get you a bath and get ready for bed." I said softly as I walked over to her. She looked at Fury and he smiled, nodding to her to go with me.

"I'll be right here. When you get out, I'll read you a bedtime story." He said to her. He winked at me, and I took her hand and let her to the bathroom.

Emma walked into the bathroom and gasped when she saw the tub full of bubbles and toys. She stood there fidgeting for a moment and looked at me.

"Let's take your clothes off and put them in the hamper then you can play in the bath for a bit. I have your pajamas here on the counter. I'll show you when you get in." I said to her. She had her arms crossed over her chest. "Do you want me to turn around while you get undressed?"

She nodded her little head, so I turned around. When she was done, she tugged my hand. I turned slightly and helped her get into the tub. She blew the bubbles and played with the ducks while I sat on the toilet waiting for her. I really wanted her to be comfortable with me.

"So, can you tell me if there is anything you don't like to eat or may be allergic to?" I asked her as I watched her play. "I'm going to order groceries tomorrow and I wanted to be sure to get things you like."

"I don't like spinach or brussels sprouts. I like broccoli, cauliflower, green beans, carrots, corn and chicken, and hamburgers. I like lots of stuff. My mommy tried to buy different things for me to try." She said looking at the toys. "I like ice cream too, but we didn't have that much."

"Ok, so how about I make sure to get some of that and we will keep going with trying different things." I suggested looking at the time. "We should probably get you out before you turn into prune." I pulled a towel from the cabinet and held it open for her. She stood up and opened her arms for me to wrap the towel around her and pick her up. "I'm going to pat you dry, if anything I do scares you or makes you uncomfortable you need to tell me, okay?"

"Ok Ms. Lillian." She stood there and let me dry her off with the towel. I let her hold it while I handed her a pair of panties with crowns on it. She smiled and put the towel down to step into them. I then handed her a nightgown with Moana on it. She held her hands up for me to pull it over her head. "Do you like fuzzy socks?"

She smiled and nodded. I handed her a pair of striped socks with pink, purple and white. She sat down and pulled them on her feet. I watched her pick up her towel and hang it on the rack. Then she picked Sprinkles up from the counter and we went to get Fury. When we walked in, I saw him at the door to her room and his eyes were misty. He smiled at me so warmly.

"Would you like to see your room?" I asked her as I walked toward the door. She followed me and Fury opened the door all the way and flipped on the light. She looked at it with wonder on her little face and walked around touching things. I walked over and flipped on the lamp for her. She took in the toys in the basket over in the corner on the plush throw rug. The stroller, baby bed and changing table were set up. I made sure to leave room for her barbie house. She held her stuffie close to her chest and walked over to the bed. Fury turned back the cover and picked her up, sitting her on the bed. "What do you think?"

"I've never had my own room before. I used to sleep with my mommy." She said sounding a little lost. "It's so pretty."

"There is a monitor beside the bed. If you get scared at any time, just call out and one of us will be right here. The lamp will be your nightlight. Would you like your Papi to read you a bedtime story?" I asked her. She looked at the small bookshelf on the wall above her nightstand and pointed to The Velveteen Rabbit. Fury took it and sat down beside her. She scooted closer to him and laid her head against his chest as he started to read to her. I sat at the end of the bed just watching them together. If I wasn't sure I was in love with him before, I was now.

He read her the entire book, even after she was asleep, he continued to read until he finished it. Sitting it on the nightstand he gently laid her back on her pillow and pulled the covers up over her. She had her stuffie in her arms and was sleeping peacefully. I turned off the overhead light and then closed the door. I turned to look at him and he dragged me into the bathroom for a shower. We washed each other and he picked me up and fucked me against the tile wall. It was a quick joining to take off the edge. We were both so wound up from being apart and me from being worried about him. When we dried off, he led me to our bed and made love to me. Kissing me like he couldn't get enough. We lay entangled in each other's arms kissing and caressing each other. I could not stop touching him reassuring myself he was really here and safe. I pushed him onto his back and started to kiss and lick my way down his body. I nuzzled my face against the hair on his chest and worked my way down to his enlarged cock. I breathed in his scent and wrapped my hand around the base before licking him like an ice cream cone. I loved the noises he made when he was turned on and his hands in my hair clenching as he tried not to come. I wanted him to though, so I started sucking him in earnest using my tongue on the sensitive spot just under the crown.

"Baby I'm gonna cum down your throat if you don't stop. I grabbed his ass and held him to me. He jetted down my throat and I licked him clean before crawling back up his body to kiss him. "Damn baby, just damn."

"I love you, Brian Nash." I told him as I looked him in the eye. He smiled and squeezed me tight against him.

"I love you to Lillian Becks. I had not planned to do it like this, but will you marry me?" he asked as he looked into my eyes. I started to cry and shook my head yes. "Use your words baby."

"Yes, you crazy stubborn man. I will marry you. Besides we have a daughter to raise together now." I giggled as I kissed him again. I guess he recovered since he flipped me over and went down on me. Showing me with his mouth, tongue and fingers how much he desired me. When he had me biting into my hand to keep from screaming, he flipped me on my hands and knees then drove his cock into me. I started coming and had to push my face into my pillow. He kept working my clit with his fingers while he fucked me from behind.

"Come again for me baby. I want to feel you as I come." He demanded sending me over the edge with him. When he pulled out, he went to get a damp cloth to clean us up pulling on a pair of sweatpants and then threw me his shirt before pulling me into his arms. "I figured we shouldn't sleep nude with a little one in the house. Just in case she wakes up."

"Probably right. She is such a sweet little thing. I hope she will be happy here. I know it will take time for her to get over losing her mother." I said running my fingers up and down his chest.

"How do you feel about us tying the knot next weekend so we can get the paperwork filed to adopt her officially?" he asked me.

"I'm good with that. I know we need to do what we can to be sure she is safe and taken care of. I've had a big wedding I just want you." I told him as I started to doze off. He continued to run his hand through my hair until I fell asleep.

16

Fury

We woke up to screams. Jumping out of the bed we ran into Emma's room, and she was thrashing around on the bed screaming. I didn't want to frighten her more, so I let Lillian approach her and I talked to her from the end of her bed.

"Poppet wake up, it's Papi and Lily. You're safe, nobody is going to hurt you." I said softly and slowly as Lily rubbed her little back trying to soothe her. She blinked her eyes wiping at the tears and looked up at me. Her little hands reaching for me, I went and picked her up sitting her in my lap.

"Papi, where is my mommy. She was hurt and bleeding everywhere?" she mumbled into my chest. My heart broke for her. It would take time for her little mind to process what she had been through and seeing her mother murdered was going to be hard.

"Remember little one, she is in heaven with the angels. She would want you to be safe and happy." I said to her as I rocked her in my arms. Emma calmed down so I laid her back against her pillow and handed her Sprinkles. She hugged the stuffie to her chest and closed her eyes. Lillian was sitting beside her running her fingers through her hair when Emma turned over and wrapped her fingers around Lily's hand and held on for a minute. When we were sure she was back asleep we got up and went to our room.

"I wish I could make it better for her. I can't imagine losing my mother at her age. It was hard enough losing my parents at sixteen." Lillian said as she crawled back into bed and curled up to my chest.

"I know baby, it will take time, but it will eventually get easier. She has both of us and all of our friends as family too." I told her as I held her close. "I won't be going anywhere until we find out where Viper and his buddy are. I'll have to neutralize that threat sooner rather than later."

"I know, I just want you to promise to take backup and be careful. We can't lose you. Emma and I need you." She told me as she snuggled closer. I put my arms around her and closed my eyes. It had been a really long day for all of us.

The next morning, I woke up and the bed beside me was empty. Clearly Lillian was already up making breakfast. I glanced at the clock and saw it was almost ten in the morning. I never sleep this late, I guess I was really exhausted. I didn't really sleep in the hospital with Emma. I wanted to be awake in case she needed me. I rubbed my hand down my face and got up to go shower. When I was done, I got dressed and went into the living area. Lillian was showing Emma something on the computer, and they looked so cute with their heads together whispering. Lillian looked up and smiled at me.

"There is a breakfast casserole still warm in the oven. We already ate, I wanted to let you sleep as long as you could." She said as she looked back down and pointed at something on the screen. I walked over to them and kissed them both on the top of the head and went to fix myself a plate.

"Thanks babe, it smells good." I told her as I took a bite. Man, my girl could cook. I ate and watched the two of them together. Emma seemed to be warming up to her. They were looking at clothes. When I finished eating, I cleaned up and put the leftovers away. "What are we doing today?"

"Well, we need to get Emma some more clothes. I didn't buy much because I wanted to be sure I got the right size first. I also want to get her a couple of pairs of shoes." Lillian looked hopeful. Emma looked up at me with big eyes as she kept staring at the computer and then back at us.

"We can do that. I need to head over and talk to Gears about a project he is working on for me then I can take you. When we get back, I'll probably head over to the garage to help out for a couple of hours." I told them as I put on my jacket to leave. "I'll be back around lunch time. We can eat lunch out and then shop."

Emma got up and came over to me. She looked a little nervous about me leaving. I hated that look but she needed to get used to being with Lillian during the day and when I was gone on missions. I squatted down in front of her and pulled her to me.

"Ok poppet, I need you to go make sure your new toys all feel welcome. I bet that baby doll in your room needs a name too." He said, looking her in the eye. She smiled and glanced toward the room my girl had fixed up for her. I knew there was a barbie house in the garage for me to put together. I would do that before I went to bed tonight. "Can you do that?"

She nodded and gave me a hug before carrying her stuffie to the room to play. Lillian came over and put her arms around me. I pulled her in for a kiss.

"I'll be back in a bit. It will be fine." I told her as I kissed her nose then headed out. I waited until she closed the door then I headed over to the clubhouse.

I walked in the front door and headed straight for Axle's office. We had planned to meet up around eleven to see what Gears had found on Viper. I knocked and heard him bark out 'come in'. Opening the door, I saw him sitting behind his desk with a cup of coffee and a frown. Gears wasn't there yet.

"Gears called he will be here in a few minutes. How is the girl doing?" he asked. Axle had seen the attachment firsthand. He knew that we were going to adopt her.

"She's doing as well as can be expected after seeing her mother murdered and being kidnapped by traffickers. She had a nightmare last night, but we were able to get her back to sleep. It's going to be one day at a time." I told him as I sat down on one of the chairs. "Lillian has agreed to marry me, we are going to do it here if that is okay. Nothing big, she said she has had big, and we just want to be married and get the adoption process started."

"Congrats man, I know you had your eye on her for a long time. You have had a lot of patience waiting for her to be ready to move on. I'm glad you have each other." Axle said as Gears tapped and opened the door. Laptop in hand as usual.

"Hey guys, sorry I was checking a couple of leads." He sat down in the chair closest to the desk and set up his laptop. "Where is everyone else?"

"This meeting is just us; we will have everyone come in later if needed." Axle said as Gears pulled up the footage he had.

"You had me looking at cameras around the areas that Viper frequents in Boston as well as the cameras around here using the facial recognition software. We got a hit. He was spotted the night before last at his favorite little bar in Southie. His buddy was with him. I reached out to some of our contacts there and found out they were heading out of town yesterday. I haven't seen anything or heard a peep since. I would suggest keeping a close watch on the girls until we do." Gears looked disgusted. "Every contact we have has confirmed that they are the only two remaining from the Boston chapter. If we can find them, we can close that chapter for good. I know O'Leary is looking for them too."

"I'd love to get my hands on them and take care of them personally. I want to hurt them and watch them die in front me." I said as I played with one of my knives. My chain was gone, and I wanted a replacement. Both of my brothers looked at me and Axle raised his eyebrow. "What, you think just because I have a family now that I'm not the same guy?"

"Does Lillian know his ass is bat shit crazy?" Gears asked with a laugh. "You really are something Fury."

"She knows what she is getting. Lillian was an old lady in this club before and she is going to be one again. She doesn't ask questions that she knows we can't answer, and she helps where she can when she can." I rubbed the back of my neck and got up. "I'm taking the girls shopping. Em needs more clothes and shoes. I need someone else to go along and keep an eye out."

"I'll have Hawk follow you. You know he would be pissed if we didn't let him watch your back." Axle picked up his phone and shot off a text to Hawk. I just nodded.

"Ok, let me know if you hear anything else. Thanks guys." I said as I walked out the door. This club had been my family for as long as I can remember. My half brother was also in it. We were not especially close as his mother had run off with him when he was a baby. He found me and the club a few years ago. Axle let him be a prospect until he earned his cut. I really needed to try more with the kid.

Walking up to my door I saw Emma look out the window, so I waved to her. She smiled and waved back. I opened the door, and she wrapped her little arms around my leg. I reached down and picked her up, giving her a hug. I looked over at Lillian as she came out of the bathroom with her hair fixed and a little makeup on. She was so beautiful I just stared for a few minutes. Smiling, she walked over and tiptoed to kiss me.

"Emma, can you go put your shoes on?" I asked her as I sat her back down. Lillian put her arm around my waist.

"She hasn't stopped watching the door since you left. I think she was scared you weren't coming back." Lillian told me quietly. "It's going to take a while for her to realize that we won't abandon her. I'm really glad that I work from home. I messaged Bethann and asked her to bring the boys here for me to keep from now on. She understood and she's fine with it."

Emma came back out of her room with her boots on. She had her stuffie in her arms. "I'm ready." she said quietly. We slipped on our coats and headed out. I noticed Hawk following behind us from a distance. I was thankful for my brothers. I wanted my girls to be able to enjoy their shopping and I would feel better knowing there was another set of eyes keeping watch.

"Let's just hit Walmart today. We can get shoes, clothes and snacks there. I placed a grocery order to pick up already." Lillian suggested. I know she was trying to keep the trip short, and I appreciated that she was aware of the situation.

"Ok sure, we will do that and then pick up pizza on the way home." I said as I pulled into the parking lot. I found a spot near the door. I got out, opened the door for Lillian and then got Emma out of the

SUV. She held our hands and walked between us. "What kind of pizza do you like Emma?"

"Mommy used to get us the frozen kind. I like cheese and pepperoni." She said looking around the store. We headed to the little girl clothes first. Emma didn't touch anything, she just looked.

"What do you like sweetie?" Lillian asked her as she pulled a few things off the racks to show her. Emma bit her lip and looked at me then back at Lillian.

"I've never been able to pick out my own clothes. My favorite color is pink. I like dresses and jeans too." she walked over to a rack with Disney princess' dresses and shirts. She reached out to touch one then tucked her little hands behind her back.

"Baby girl, you can touch them. I want you to help pick them out. We will help make sure the sizes are right." I told her as I looked at Lillian and saw her blinking back tears. I want you to pick out ten outfits. You will need some warm clothes as well as dresses."

"Okay Papi." She said as she picked out a few things along with some dresses and pajamas. Lillian had already got her plenty of panties and socks. Next, we went and looked at the shoes. She had some cute boots already, so we looked at a pair of sneakers and some dress shoes for her. I watched her little face light up at the light up shoes and little black shoes with pink bows on the top. After we had all the clothes she needed for now I led them to the toiletries so we could be sure she had plenty of bubble bath and tear-free shampoo as well as some detangler spray for her hair. We picked up some hair ties and bows as well. Once we had the items paid for and in the back seat, we drove around to pick up our grocery order. As we were heading to the pizza place, I thought I saw Viper on his bike in my rearview mirror.

"Babe, I want you to call Hawk and tell him I need him to pick up the pizza on the way home. We are going straight back to the compound." I whispered as I handed her my phone. I glanced back and saw that Emma had fallen asleep. "I think I saw one of the guys we are looking for, so I'll feel better if we don't make any additional stops. Just tell him what you want and why."

To her credit she didn't balk or ask any questions. Lillian dialed Hawk's number and told him what we needed.

"I saw him, what do you need me to do?" Hawk answered.

"Fury asked to have you stop and pick up the pizza. We need one all meat and one pepperoni. He doesn't want us to stop until we get home." Lillian told him.

"I got it. Call me when you get home. I'll see you shortly." Hawk said before he hung up. I kept an eye on the biker in my mirror. He was following us, so I made sure he knew where we were going. We would be ready for him. As I pulled up to the gate, I nodded at Gator to let us in and jerked my head behind me letting him know we were being followed. As the gate closed behind us, we saw him drive slowly past and then keep going.

"Lily, we are going to have you, Bethann, Sophie and Annie stay at the clubhouse tonight with the kids. It will be easier to guard you all if you're in one place. We will make it seem like a big sleepover to welcome Emma to the family." I told her as we pulled into the garage. We got out and Lillian picked up Emma and I grabbed all of the shopping bags. She carried Emma and laid her on her bed, pulling off her shoes and pulling a blanket over her. Leaving her door ajar so we would hear her.

Lillian knew what we would be doing, and she knew not to ask questions. She took a duffle bag out of the hall closet and packed a bag for all of us. Since we would likely be late getting home, we would all just sleep at the clubhouse. Knowing they were here in town; Gears would be able to track them through the traffic cameras. We wanted to end this tonight. We would wait until dark and go hunting. Personally, I hoped they would come here, it would be much quicker. I sent out a group message to ensure we were all on the same page. I heard Hawk pull up outside and a few minutes later knock.

"Hey man, thanks. Come on in." I said as I opened the door and took the pizza. "I know you need to get home to get Bethann and the boys ready to go to the clubhouse later. Thank you so much for having my back today."

"Whatever, you know you don't have to thank me. That's what we do." Hawk said as he watched Lillian put stuff in the duffle bag. "Hey Lil, how are you holding up?"

"I'll feel better once those men are out of the way. Please watch this hothead of mine. We need him home safe." She winked at him. I growled and she giggled.

"I am perfectly capable of taking care of myself." I said firmly, wrapping my arm around her waist and tugging her to me. "We will make sure you are all safe."

"I know you will. I'm going to go grab whatever we need from the bathroom for the night while you talk." She said, heading into our room. I watched her and then turned to Hawk so we could discuss our plans.

17

Lillian

My hands were shaking as I gathered the things, I thought we might need for tonight. After putting it in the duffle bag I sat down on our bed and closed my eyes. I knew what I was getting into when I agreed to marry him. I also know that he is older than Wolf was and has more experience. After being taken before, he will be very cautious. I just don't want anything to happen to him. It would break me, and that little girl adores him. She hasn't quite made up her mind about me yet. I can tell, but we need more time. I have to keep a positive attitude for all of us. We were going to wait until around six thirty to go over there so we could have dinner before we got together and then put the kids to bed. They guys planned to wait until then to leave unless they bring the fight here.

I heard the door open and looked up to see Fury standing there watching me. He held his arms open, and I walked into them. I needed to be held for a bit. We slipped off our shoes and lay on the bed holding each other. Emma would be up from her nap soon.

"Baby, you know we will take every precaution. I want the threat to you both gone. These guys don't know how to organize an attack, they were just muscle. I listened while I was being beaten and tortured. I didn't speak and sometimes I pretended to be knocked out. They have no code, no morals and no decency. I'm sure this will be over tonight." He said as he rubbed my back. "Axle has already said that after this I am on a temporary leave so we can take care of our wedding, Emma's adoption and get her acclimated to being with us."

"I'm glad you brought her to live with us. I already adore that little girl. I want to spoil her rotten." I told him as he kissed me.

"I have no doubt you will do just that." He laughed and rolled to get up so that we could eat dinner. "We will have a quick planning meeting after we get over there, but we don't plan to leave until the kids are asleep."

I nodded and got up to slip my shoes back on. I walked to the door of Emma's room, and she was sitting on the floor playing with her dolls. Smiling, I headed into the kitchen to get some plates down and fix our drinks. After putting a couple of slices of pepperoni on her plate I called her to the table for dinner.

"Go wash your hands and we will have dinner." I told her. Emma nodded and went into the bathroom to wash. I had a stepstool in there so she could reach the sink better. Fury came back out of our bathroom and tweaked her nose as he put a couple of slices on his own plate. We sat down to eat dinner as a family. I thought to myself how much I had always wanted this. I had come so close to having it before only to have it snatched away from me. I prayed that it would not happen again. We ate and Emma talked a little about the shopping trip, telling us how much fun she had picking out her clothes and shoes. She was so easy to please and appreciative of what she was given. I just wanted to hold her and hug her tight. Her little eyes lit up whenever she looked at Fury and I couldn't blame her I was pretty gone on him too. I never would have expected him to make such a good father, but he was amazing with her.

"Emma, we are going to have a huge sleepover party at the clubhouse tonight. Everyone wants to welcome you to the family." He told her acting like it was no big deal. She looked at us for a minute and took another bite of her pizza. I could see the wheels turning in her head.

"Okay, will there be a bunch of people." She asked. "I'm used to being around a lot of kids. The mean lady used to keep a bunch of kids at one time, then some of them would not come back and she would find new ones." Emma frowned as she said it and her little face paled. No doubt thinking about what happened before.

"There will be several adults there and three little boys. You saw the neighborhood inside the fence when we left earlier?" I asked her and she nodded. "That is all our family. Your Papi is in a motorcycle club, and they help people. We all live inside the gates to keep us safe."

"I'm sure that Cameron, Joshua and Mattie will be excited to have another friend to play with." Fury said as he patted her hand. She smiled and finished eating her dinner. When we were finished, we had her go pick out what she wanted to bring with her. She came out with Sprinkles, her babydoll and a soft blanket.

"Are you ready?" I asked while I helped her into her coat and put mine on. Fury had warmed up the SUV for us. I would have argued that it is a short walk, but he didn't want us out in the open or getting sick. I knew the drill.

As we walked in, I saw the boys sitting on the floor playing with their cars and watching Monsters, Inc. I helped Emma remove her coat and she went over to play with them. They waved at her, and Cameron introduced them. He was such a good boy. She sat down on the floor leaning against the couch holding her stuffie and blanket. I took the doll to Fury's old room, and he put our duffle in there as well. I kept coloring books and crayons at the clubhouse for when the kids came so I got some out and brought to her along with a tray.

"Thank you." Emma said as she wrapped her stuffie up and put it beside her. I let her color and watch the movie and walked over to the kitchen to talk to the other women. I had a notebook and a pen in my hand.

"Ok ladies. Who wants to help me plan a small wedding?" I asked them and they squealed. I laughed and smiled. This is what we needed to distract us while the guys were in the conference room plotting and planning. "It's going to be small, but we wanted to have it here in the clubhouse. He hasn't had a chance to get me a ring yet. He said he is going to take care of that as soon as this is handled."

"This will be so much fun. Do you have a theme in mind or color scheme?" Sophie asked as she took a sip of wine. "I'm sure we can get this place fixed up."

"I just want a pretty dress for myself and for Emma. I want to include her in the ceremony, so she knows she is a part of this. I am thinking pink sweetheart roses with baby's breath for my bouquet and a pink dress for her. I just want something cute. I can also have a pink dress since I have been married before. I told Fury that he can wear whatever he wants. I just want to do this and then have a party to celebrate." I told them as I looked over at Emma and Cam talking to each other. He was so cute to her. "I think Cam is smitten."

Bethann laughed and agreed. We watched them as he sat on her other side, and she shared her coloring book and crayons with him. "Oh boy, I think that is a friendship in the making there." We all laughed and didn't hear the guys come out of the room. Fury came up behind me and wrapped his arms around my waist.

"What's so funny?" he asked, and I jerked my head toward the kids. I felt him stiffen up. "Hmmm, he doesn't need to sit that close to her."

"Oh hush, they are just kids. Leave them alone. You can worry about that in about ten years." I said elbowing him gently in the ribs. He chuckled in my ear and bit it. "Neanderthal" I said smiling. We sat on one of the couches and cuddled until I noticed Emma's eyes drooping.

"Let's get you ready for bed Emma." I said as I stood up and picked her up. She held her stuffie and threw her blanket over her as I carried her to the room. We took off her clothes and put on her pajamas. After she went to the potty and brushed her teeth, she laid on the bed and Fury read her a story. Once she was asleep, I turned on the bathroom light and left the door ajar. Then we went back to the common room.

18

Fury

During our meeting, Gears told us that they were holed up down the road in an abandoned house. We had a couple of prospects keeping an eye on them to let us know if they left. The plan was to box them in and take them out. He confirmed there were only two of them. I was guessing they were here for revenge. Since they were wanted in several states, we talked about turning them in. I just wasn't sure I was willing to let them keep breathing. They had planned to kill me and would have given the chance. Viper had enjoyed working me over while I was tied to a chair.

We knew we had them outnumbered but we didn't know what kind of firepower they had in that house. We were going to approach in pairs. We were all dressed in black with earpieces to stay in contact. Hawk suggested we try to lure them out of the house. I just wanted this over and done. When I first woke up all I could think of was returning the favor, but now I just wanted to go home to my girls. I didn't want to have to explain bloody knuckles to a four-year-old. Dog and Flapper were close by. They were prospects about to earn their patch. I made it over to where Flapper was watching the house.

"Still just the two of them?" I asked him. He nodded and pointed toward the window in the back. I saw it rise and one of the guys climb out. I couldn't tell which one it was, but I made sure Rider and Fang knew. They got him before he could make a sound. Now there was just one in the house. Axle tossed in a cannister of tear gas at the same time Blade tossed one in the back. A few minutes later the other one came stumbling out of the front coughing and wiping his eyes cussing. They grabbed him too. Dog and Flapper put their gas masks on and went through clearing the house. Once it was clear we all left to meet up at Trixie's. We had a back entrance that led down to our "guest" room. It was soundproof with a drain in the floor for easy cleanup.

Walking in I saw them tied to a chair. I popped my neck, and my knuckles and Axle handed me a chain like the one I used to have. I wrapped it around my neck and smiled. Ah, now I'm ready. I looked them over. Viper I recognized; the other guy I think I had seen in the basement a couple of times. Viper, I knew was the one who hit me over the head and helped Snake torture me. I decided to work over Viper first so we could scare the other guy.

"I see you managed to survive the fire, asshole." Viper spit out. I took the end of my chain and hit him in the leg with it. He screamed and looked at me with hatred in his eyes. "I guess we didn't hurt you enough."

"My turn." I said as I took the chain again and used it to break his tibia. He screamed again. "How does that feel, I think I need to crack a few ribs." I used it again to hit his ribcage and he was cursing, sweating and swaying with pain.

"What the fuck do you want?" Viper hissed at me. "The damn Irish killed our whole club, if Scooby and I had been there we would have been toast too."

"Scooby?? You call him Scooby? Poor bastard what a road name." I laughed and the guys all laughed with me. I glanced over and Axle looked bored playing with his phone, Blade yawned and crossed his arms over his chest. Hawk was waiting for his turn. "I think my buddy wants to get in a few. Hawk?"

"Damn straight. You think it's cool to hit my best friend upside the head, kidnap him and beat him within an inch of his life. Fuck you." Hawk said as he took his knife and started to carve into the man's neck. He started begging and screaming again. "You thought it was a good idea to be Snake's pet torturer. Wrong move asshole." Hawk grabbed his hand and held it on the arm of the chair then chopped off a couple of fingers. The other guy looked like he was ready to pass out.

"You have anything to say Scooby?" I asked him as I walked over to him. His eyes got wide as he took in my height and build not to mention the blood dripping off of my chains. "You want some of this?"

"No man, please. I never touched you. I'm just an errand boy for them. Viper threatened to kill me if I didn't stay with him." Scooby said as I stepped closer and removed the chain from my neck, he wet himself.

"Damn, really? I'm glad we have a drain." Fang said from the corner of the room in disgust. "How are you going to call yourself a Ripper and you can't even control your damn bladder. Ugh."

"You know, now that we've roughed him up, we can't really let them go." Axle said as he looked at the two men. "I mean we can't have any witnesses."

"You're right. I think they need to take a dive off a cliff, how about you Fury?" Hawk asked as he flipped his knife around.

"Yeah, I'm thinking a snapped neck and then the fall should take care of it. Leave them for the bears and wolves to feed off of." Fury said as he knocked Viper out cold. Then he walked over and did the same to the other guy. "Let's get this done. Doc, you and Flapper get this cleaned up and then head home."

We threw the men in the back of one of the SUVs on some plastic and headed to the mountain pass. I planned to use a couple of sharp rocks to make sure they bled out when they hit the bottom. They would die of blood loss and exposure. It was close to midnight when we got to the highway drop off. There was not another vehicle in sight. We got out and pulled them out of the back. I took one of the sharp rocks near the edge and made sure to hit some major arteries before tossing them over. I watched until I couldn't see them anymore. After we put the plastic on the gravel and burned it.

We got home at around two in the morning. We hit the showers in the gym first and changed into some fresh clothes that we left there. After we went to our rooms.

I quietly opened the door and saw Emma between Lillian and the wall. I slipped off my shoes and crawled into bed pulling Lily closer to me. Taking a deep whiff of her scent I closed my eyes to sleep. She squeezed the hand and her waist, and I heard her mumble 'love you' before falling back asleep. I went to sleep with a smile on my face. My girls were safe, I was getting married, and life was good.

19

Lillian

A few days after they got home Bethann offered to watch Emma so we could have a night out together. Cameron and Emma were inseparable. They were the best of friends, so she was good staying with them. I took her over to their place and then went back home to get ready for our date. I took a long hot shower, shaved everything, washed my hair and then dried my hair and fixed it. I had laid out my clothes on the bed. I went and put on the lacy thong I had picked out along with a matching bra. I decided to wear a sweater dress and some thigh high boots because it was still cold out and I didn't know what he had planned.

I walked into the living room and saw Fury standing there looking hot as fuck! I really just wanted to strip his clothes off and lick him all over. Damn my man was fine. Those muscles, tats and dimples did me in every time. He looked at me and whistled. When he saw my expression, he laughed.

"See something you like baby?" he asked as he came closer. He was wearing some fitted jeans and a sweater that matched his green eyes.

I felt myself melt and I knew my thong was soaked. I stood on tiptoe and slid my arms around his neck bringing him down to me.

"You bet I do, now kiss me." I said as I licked my lips, and he took possession of my mouth. After a super-hot kiss, he pulled back and shook his head grinning at me.

"We are absolutely having this date before I strip that dress off and fuck you within an inch of your life baby. Now grab your coat so we can go." He said as he smacked my ass. I squealed and jumped looking over my shoulder to see the mischief in his eyes.

He helped me put on my coat and then held the door for me. We drove for a while, and I realized he had taken us to The Lookout in a nearby town. It was a very upscale restaurant that was known for having great food. We stopped and the valet opened the door for me. Fury came around and offered me his arm tossing the keys to the kid to park the car. We walked in and the hostess gave him the once over like she was sizing him up for dinner.

"We have a reservation for two under the name Brian Nash." He said to the hostess. She then noticed that he had his arm around me. Taking a couple of menus, she handed them to a server and told them where to seat us.

He had called ahead and told them he wanted a seat near the window. The place was well heated with several fireplaces around the room. The table we got had one close to it and had an amazing view of the snow-covered mountains. He held the chair for me as I sat down then he pulled his close to me. The waiter came over and Fury ordered us a bottle of wine.

"What would you like to eat love?" he asked me as we looked at the menu. There were no prices. I had never been anywhere like this before. "Whatever you like."

"I want the seafood pasta and a salad." I told him as the waiter came back. Fury ordered for both of us and then we were left alone. "This place is lovely, thank you for bringing me here."

"You deserve a great date baby. We never really got one." He said as he held my hand. I noticed he was staring at me and suddenly he stood up and got down on one knee by my chair. He pulled a ring box out of his pocket and opened it. Inside sat a beautiful princess-cut diamond on a wide yellow gold band. "Lillian Jade Becks, will you do me the honor of marrying me. Be my wife and my old lady for the rest of our days?"

I teared up and threw my arms around his neck kissing him. When we broke apart, he smiled at me. "Baby, use your words. Is that a, yes?"

"Yes, of course yes. I love you so much and I'd love to have you as my husband and old man." I cried and held him close. He slid the ring on my finger and kissed me again then sat back in his seat in time for our waiter to bring our wine and pour us a glass. I could not stop looking from him at my ring and back at him. This gorgeous man loves me and wants to marry me. He made me a mom and I have never been so happy in my life. We finished our meal and got dessert to go. I wanted to be home alone with my fiancé. We were walking back to the front when the hostess handed him a folded-up piece of paper. He looked at her and handed it back.

"This is my girl right here. See the ring on her finger, we are engaged. It was very rude of you to try to make a pass at me when I am clearly here with someone. I'll be speaking to your manager." Fury said as he put his arm around my shoulders and walked us out. The valet brought the car around and he held open my door then reached in to buckle me up. Kissing me on the nose before he closed the door to get in on the driver's side. I was absolutely on cloud nine. I loved that he called her out and didn't allow her to disrespect me that way.

He took my hand and placed it on his thigh and drove us home. He held onto my hand the entire way. We had already set the date of the wedding for next Saturday it was supposed to warm up in the next week. I couldn't wait. When we got home Fury came around and opened my door and then pulled me into the house. We hung our coats on the hooks by the door and he threw me over his shoulder and started for our room. I was giggling at first but when he slid his hand up my thigh under my dress and ripped off my wet thong I moaned. Standing me up beside the bed he lifted my leg and unzipped my boot peeling it off, then he did the same with the other one. I reached down and pulled the dress over my head, and he unclasped my bra. Suddenly I was standing there naked while he was still fully dressed. I pouted.

"That's not fair." I said as I reached to help him pull off his sweater and undershirt. Then I reached for his fly as he kicked off his shoes. I undid his pants peeling them away from his massive erection and licked my lips. He growled at me as I wrapped my hand around the base and took the crown into my mouth. I looked up at him as I took him down my throat and hummed. I felt the tremble in his thighs and kept working him. I pushed his pants down his legs as I kept him in my mouth, and he stepped out of them. I ran my hands up his muscled torso and moaned around his cock. I raised up to lick around the head and suck on it. He eased me off of him and flipped me over.

"Hands and knees on the bed, now!" he demanded. I did as he said. He used his thumbs to spread me open for his tongue as he ate me from behind. Every dip and lick brought me closer to the edge. I knew I didn't have to be quiet because Emma wasn't home. He slipped a finger in and started fucking me with it while flicking my clit when I flew apart. Next thing I knew he pulled me to the edge of the bed and thrust inside me. He held me still for a minute to get control before he started using my hips to fuck me hard. He was hitting a spot deep inside me that had me wailing with pleasure and suddenly I was there again, and he went with me. He kept an arm around my waist and kissed my spine. Oh my God, I get this for the rest of my life. What a lucky girl I am. I giggled to myself. He snagged some tissues from beside the bed to clean us up. We dozed off but he woke me up several times during the night to take me again. Once we ate the dessert off of each other and had to shower. It was the best night of my life.

20

Fury

It was our wedding day, almost spring. The days were getting a little warmer and I couldn't wait to take my girl for a ride on the back of my bike. I had taken her around the property a few times, but it had been too cold for a longer ride. I didn't want her to get sick. I got up and showered and went in search of coffee in my sweats. There were no kids in the clubhouse today, just me and the single guys. I will be getting dressed for the wedding soon. I stepped out into the common room and was again amazed at how they had transformed the space for our special day. There were two small rows of chairs lined up with bows tied to the chairs on the inside of the little aisle they created. There were decorations on the table for the wedding feast, the women had been cooking up a storm. I could not wait to see my girls in their dresses.

"So, it's your turn to take the long walk." Hawk teased as he came in mostly dressed. "I figured I better get over here and make sure you are ready. Bethann shooed me so she could go help Lillian and Emma get ready. Annie is watching the boys and bringing them with her and Undertaker."

"Ha, ha. I seem to remember you doing this not too long ago." I teased him. Hawk just smiled. He absolutely adored Bethann. She was good to him.

"I'd do it again every day." He said as he clapped me on the back. "You best go get dressed. You have the rings?"

I handed him the box that held our wedding bands. We had a local minister coming to perform the ceremony. Lillian and I had secured our license a few days ago. It was almost ten and the ceremony was going to be at noon so I went to grab something to eat and drink my coffee so I could go get ready.

It was about eleven thirty when I came back out of the room dressed and ready. I saw that almost everyone was there. Bethann winked at me and pointed to the office. So, my girls were here also. Everyone was getting seated, and the minister took his place. Hawk came over and pinned on a boutonniere to match the one he was wearing. He was my best man. Bethann was going to be Lillian's maid of honor and Emma our flower girl. The first song played, and I got into place. Then Bethann was next followed by Emma who looked completely adorable in her frilly pink dress holding a basket of rose petals. She beamed as she walked down dropping the petals until she stood beside Bethann. Pachelbel's Canon started playing and everyone stood as Lillian came to stand at the end of the aisle being walked down by Zeke 'Undertaker'. She looked like a vision wearing a pale pink lace A-line dress with pale pink heels and her lovely dark hair curled around her face. She looked stunning. She was holding a small bouquet of pink roses with baby's breath mixed in. As the music played, she walked down to me. The minister asked the question, and her hands were placed in mine. We stood there and made our vows in front of our family. That's what they were. We had a family of our own making. When it came time for the exchanging of rings Hawk held open the box for us to take them out. After we were pronounced husband and wife Axle came up to us and handed me another box. It was a white box with our logo on it. I held it for her to open. Lillian blinked up at me and smiled. She raised the lid, and I pulled the cut out of the box. I handed the empty box to Axle and helped her put the cut on. Axle said a few words about her always being a part of the club and that she was the beating heart of one of the members etc. etc. She cried and I handed her the tissue from my pocket. I knew she was also remembering her wedding to Wolf. I hated that he had to die, but I was grateful that I got to spend my life with her.

We kissed and I picked her up and carried her down the aisle. Setting her down I turned and held out my arms to Emma who ran down the aisle to us. She jumped into my arms, and I held her. We had our first dance as husband and wife, then I danced with Emma and Lillian danced with Hawk. As we sat down for the wedding feast, I noticed that Fang's younger sister Katherine was here, and she was sitting beside Rider looking way too cozy. I wasn't sure what that was about but today it was not my problem. I glanced over at my friend who was giving Rider a look. I guess we would see how this played out. Today all I cared about was being with my wife and daughter.

Emma was coming out of her shell. She still had nightmares occasionally, but they were less frequent. She loved Lillian and had started calling her Mama, saying that Mommy would always be for her other mom. We were about to make a champagne toast when Lillian smiled and put her hand over her glass. She pulled out a small bottle of apple juice and poured it in her glass. Winking at me she toasted to our future.

"You're pregnant?" I asked looking at my beautiful wife. She nodded and smiled. Looking down at Emma, I asked her. "Em, how do you feel about being a big sister?" She squealed and nodded her head excited by the news. Looks like I got more than one gift today.

The End.

Also By

Some books include the Also By information on the same page as the author bio, but many have a separate page dedicated to sharing more works by the same author or publishing house that the reader might be interested. This page can be a very powerful marketing tool.

The text on this page is typically center aligned.

Printed in Great Britain
by Amazon